Neon Lights and Natural Satellites

a playlist

ISBN 979-8-218-49370-7

Book cover images and design by Colton Myhre
Author photograph by Jack Villalobos

Published by Mt. Dupere Publishing

Neon Lights and Natural Satellites

a playlist

(a novel)

By Colton Myhre

Intro:
"400 Lux"
by Lorde

JD sat outside against the wall of the music building listening to the deafening sounds of the Wind Symphony Orchestra permeating through the red bricks. He knew he should be in there playing with them, but his body wouldn't move. JD was not a rule breaker, and he didn't miss concerts—especially on purpose—but he stayed seated. He closed his eyes and mirrored the notes with his hand as if playing along. He was beyond prepared for the concert. He had the program memorized; it was dedicated to famous American composers, which was a fitting theme for a concert on the Fourth of July.

JD continued to follow along to the sounds of the Souza march bouncing out from the concert hall. The song was ending soon, and the Gershwin would start. He knew he should be in there, but he couldn't bear the thought of playing alongside Arjun again. He couldn't bear to hear Arjun play another solo.

He peeled himself off the concrete, picked up his French horn in its sleek, black case, and started to walk home to his dorm. He trudged, kicking small rocks and scuffing his polished dress shoes. Normally he would care, but today he didn't. He was furious at Arjun. Dating the best French horn player at the university was good in theory, except that JD was the second-best French horn player. After their fight, JD planned on walking back in to play at the concert. He planned on taking his seat next to Arjun, saying nothing, and playing the show, but when the time came, JD couldn't do it. He sat outside of the building as the concert started.

Despite the growing distance from the music building, JD felt like he could still hear the bright, brassy sounds coming from the concert. He wondered if the chair next to Arjun had been left empty, or if they removed it before the curtain; JD couldn't tell which scenario made him angrier. Bitterly, he reached into his pocket and pulled out his headphones. He played the first song that came up.

JD was relieved to drown out the sounds of the concert. He had never ditched a performance in his life. He had nightmares about forgetting his instrument, but he never did. It's impossible to forget your instrument when you practice every day. JD thought about Dr. Cleary. She must have noticed by now that one of the two French horn players was missing. But then again, JD thought, she must be relieved that it was him and not Arjun missing. Missing the second French horn part is noticeable to her, the conductor, but missing a soloist would ruin a show. JD thought of excuses to tell Dr. Cleary in an email or on Monday, but it put a pit in his stomach. She would see right through him. It had been JD's dream for almost a decade to study music at Larimer University and be a composer. There was nothing he wanted more or worked harder for, but now that he was here, his dream had somehow become something miserable in this first year of college. He thought this summer ensemble class would be nice, but when Arjun decided to take it too, it felt like how the whole year had been. JD walked faster.

The next song played through JD's headphones, and it reminded him of Arjun. Not the Arjun playing a solo in the concert, or the Arjun that was probably furious with JD right now, but the Arjun that, two years ago, had kissed JD for the first time. He remembered it vividly. Arjun had driven JD to an overlook just outside of town. JD sat in the passenger seat and admired the sunset over the mountains. The dramatic display of dying light poured sunbeams into the car and made the cracks in the windshield glisten. JD remembered the way he looked over at Arjun and couldn't help but stare. Arjun had dark, curly hair piled messily on top of his head and a sharp-bridged nose that curved downward. When Arjun kissed him, every movement was so slow and gentle that it felt like the sun had stopped setting, and just rested on the horizon—waiting and glowing. JD remembered thinking that some people never get kissed like that. Some people never get to feel things like that.

JD stopped at a bench near the edge of campus. He sat down and let the rest of the song play before taking out his headphones. He wished for a moment that he could go back in time. He thought about it and decided that he would go back to his junior year of high school. He'd met Arjun during band camp, and they were instantly friends. It was exciting to meet someone as excited about music as JD was, but what was most exciting was falling in love for the first time. JD didn't know what changed when they went to college together, but it wasn't the same.

The nostalgia was sweet, and JD thought again about the memory in Arjun's car. The memory of his boyfriend's face bathed in orange glow didn't fade from JD's mind, but instead, stuck like hot sugar and burned as it lingered. JD felt silly to resent his own boyfriend for being a better musician, but it was all JD heard every time he listened to himself practice. No matter how much he practiced, he would never sound better or write better music than Arjun. For all of his first year of college, JD couldn't get himself to write anything good, and he hated hearing the beautiful pieces that Arjun showcased each month. JD often wondered if he'd resent Arjun more or less if he wasn't dating him. It was an ugly thought, but it was interrupted by the ringing of JD's phone. He looked down and saw Arjun's name. It must be intermission. He answered it.

"Hello?"

"What the hell, JD? Where are you?"

"What?"

"What do you mean 'what?' I can't believe you just left!"

JD fumbled his words, "I just—"

"Just what?" Arjun snapped.

The words spilled out of JD's mouth, "I'm just sick and tired of you acting like you're better than everyone?"

"What? Don't put this on me! You played a wrong note during the warm-up, and I corrected you. It's not a big deal!"

JD didn't say anything. He wanted to argue. He wanted to show Arjun how angry he was, but he just felt silly. It shouldn't have been a big deal. Being corrected for playing something wrong isn't a big deal, but when Arjun said it, JD couldn't help but feel like he said it loud enough for everyone around them to hear. Like he wanted everyone to know that he deserved the solo over JD. It made JD's blood boil.

"It's just the intermission; are you at least coming back for the Copland?" Arjun waited a moment, but JD's silence answered for him. "JD," Arjun's voice stumbled. "Please."

JD was silent.

"You're not, are you? I can't believe you. God, JD, you are so fucking selfish!" He hung up.

The silence was stale in the air as JD lowered the phone from his ear. He was stunned by the words. He thought about calling back, or texting, but he didn't. The pit in his stomach grew. JD knew that he should have gone back. He knew that he should be playing the concert, but JD also knew that he wouldn't be able to make it back in time—even if he wanted to.

The harshness of Arjun's words rang in JD's ears. He had never heard Arjun like that. He thought about the boy in the car with the dark gentle eyes and kind smile. He thought about all the warmth he'd ever heard in Arjun's voice. Thinking about that tenderness eroding away slowly, or crashing down in a wave from one terrible blow made JD ache. He didn't know which it was, but he did know that he was the one who'd caused it.

The late afternoon sun was hot and bright as JD continued the walk to his dorm; the reflection on the pavement hurt his eyes. He tried to take in the verdant greens and red brick of campus, but JD's mood soured the view. He had planned on spending the summer practicing and composing pieces in preparation for the fall semester; he wanted to go into his second year of college feeling confident with a new, strong portfolio, but everything he wrote felt wrong. Every piece felt like a practice piece that isn't meant to be shared with anyone, or like an echo of pieces already written. He had nothing to show for all the time he'd spent in practice rooms. Nothing to show for a full year of being a Music Composition Major. Nothing to prove that he deserved to be there. JD thought the quietness of campus during the summer would help, but instead just felt lonely. He spent most evenings with Arjun, but rarely just the two of them. Arjun's friends stayed for the summer as well, and that somehow also made it all feel lonelier.

JD sat on a bench and tried to admire the tall elm trees lining the sidewalk, and the noble stone columns that fortified and decorated some of the older buildings. JD wanted so badly to love college. Everything about campus and the Music Composition program had exceeded his expectations. Everything impressed JD, except for himself. JD opened his phone and paused the music. He opened the PDF of his most recent composition and stared at it. He followed the notes and let the melody play in his head. He knew how it sounded by heart; he'd played it on the piano a thousand times. What he couldn't figure out is how it should sound. He tried to rework it, to add or change what it might need, but every time he tried, he ended up with the same dull, singsong tune just with different notes. JD had spent hours on this piece getting nowhere, and looking at it again, JD felt even more dejected. He couldn't help but feel like being a composer was impossible, at least for him. He felt like whatever was inside him in high school that wrote beautiful music and loved it had somehow left. Like he'd spent all of his talent and inspiration too soon.

JD's phone buzzed in his hand. He expected to see Arjun's name again, but it wasn't. JD was about to ignore the email notification but noticed that it was from Dr. Cleary. JD looked at the time. Dr. Cleary must have written the email just as the concert ended. Nervously, JD read the message:

Subject: Dismissal from the Undergraduate Music Composition Program.

Dear JD Miller,

Due to recent lack of adherence to our attendance policy, I am sorry to inform you of your immediate dismissal from the Undergraduate Music Composition Program here at Larimer University. If you would like to appe—

He stopped reading, but anger overpowered his disbelief and he continued.

If you would like to appeal this decision, please contact the College of Fine Arts admissions office.

JD was furious. He worked harder than anyone in that building and had never missed even a rehearsal before. Feverishly, JD drafted a response asking if it was a mistake, but the response was short and quick:

JD,

I'm sorry, but the Composition Program is an incredibly competitive Major. If you would like to appeal this decision, please contact the College of Arts admissions office.

The email was a punch in the gut. The hours spent practicing seemed to mock him. The time spent writing and rewriting music felt like a cruel joke. This couldn't be it. She couldn't do this. JD stared at the short, dismissive email and let fester the reality that Dr. Cleary could and did. JD buried the phone in his pocket. He had heard of others that got kicked out of the composition program, but they didn't care. Not as much as JD. They didn't work for it.

JD's chest felt like it was on fire. He stood up, grabbed his French horn case, and began walking back down the sidewalk. As he passed the brick buildings, he thought about coming up with a lie about why he left, but he figured that word must already have reached Dr. Cleary; word that JD had stormed off after getting corrected for a wrong note. JD was flooded with embarrassment. When he thought about appealing the decision, he was furious, but thinking about telling Arjun made him want to cry. JD hated the thought that Arjun already knew about the email or was the one who told Dr. Cleary what had happened.

All year, JD felt like he couldn't measure up to Arjun, that Arjun was the only one fulfilling that dream they both had always had. Now it was official. Anger and humiliation welled in JD's hands, and, without thinking, JD gripped the handle of his French horn case, and threw it as hard as he could at the brick wall next him. He expected to hear a loud crack from the plastic case, or even a clang from the brass instrument itself, but instead heard a THUMP followed by a crash and a bellow as the instrument case careened into a passing cyclist, hurling him off the bike into the grass.

A new wave of more immediate shame and embarrassment poured over JD. Messy tears and sobs broke free.

"What the hell??" the cyclist yelped.

"I'm— I'm—" the sobs corked each syllable.

The deep furrow in the cyclist's brow melted instantly into a look of true pity. "Woah, dude…"

"I'm sor—" JD muttered.

"Hey, man, it is all good. I'm fine," he said, picking up his bike.

Humiliated and still somehow angry, JD turned to leave, walking quickly towards the dorms. JD thought to look back, but instead stared down at the concrete as he walked up the street, almost at the jog.

It wasn't thirty seconds before JD heard a voice come up next to him.

"Hey!" It was the cyclist. "You forgot this!" He rode on the street next to JD, steering with one hand, holding the French horn with the other. They stopped, and JD sheepishly took the instrument.

"I'm really sorry. I don't know what came over me."

"No, it's okay. It's fine, really."

"I'm really really sorry." JD said. The tears welled and JD looked down as he wiped snot with his tuxedo sleeve.

The cyclist got off his bike and walked it over to JD. "Are *you* okay?" He stood about two feet away from JD, and both worriedly and confusedly, patted JD's shoulder the way one would console a pouting child.

"Yeah, I'm good," JD lied, pathetically.

"Bad concert?"

JD nodded.

"I hope your instrument is okay," the boy said, gesturing to JD's French horn.

"It doesn't matter," JD said, "I won't be playing it ever again."

The boy's face hardened. "Wait, why?"

JD looked at him. The boy was wearing a dark blue helmet and a green LU shirt. He was a couple inches taller than JD, even with JD standing on the curb. "It doesn't matter. It's fine."

"The concert couldn't have been that bad."

JD smiled weakly. He turned and started to walk to his dorm.

"Were you serious when you said you'd never play again?"

The concern in the boy's voice surprised JD. It felt odd to admit the fact that it was true, but as anger fizzled away, the sadness in the statement settled in. "Yeah, I'm serious."

The boy didn't say anything for a minute. He seemed to be thinking about what to say. JD wanted to walk away again but didn't. "You know, I feel like you need, like, a cup of tea or something."

JD started to shake his head.

"Or like a muffin. Something warm," he continued.

"No really, I'm good."

"There's a coffee shop just up this street; right off campus. You can't make a decision like that on an empty stomach. Come on. It's on me."

JD, slightly bewildered, looked up at the cyclist. "*I* hit *you*, remember?"

The cyclist laughed and said, "I just think you shouldn't give up music just because you hit some guy on a bike."

"It's not that—" JD tried to correct, but he saw the smirk on the boy's face.

"C'mon, I insist." Before JD could protest again, the two of them were walking down the street. "I'm Joe by the way." They shook with each of their free hands.

"I'm JD."

"Color"
by Finish Ticket

JD and Joe walked for about five minutes before turning into a cobblestone alley. The wide alley was lined by large ceramic planters and was covered by wires of lights unlit against the afternoon blue sky. The coffee shop at the end of the alley was an eccentric, almost lopsided two-story building. There was a sign hanging about the outdoor staircase that had a painted image of a cat drinking a cup of coffee and the words, *Always open… really!*

Joe saw JD looking and asked, "have you ever been here?"

JD shook his head.

"It's pretty quirky. My girlfriend showed it to me a couple years ago. The best part is that they mean it—they're always open—twenty-four hours a day, and apparently even on the Fourth of July."

JD kept forgetting it was the Fourth and wondered if Joe had other plans he'd rather be at. Joe locked his bike up, and the two of them climbed the steps. The air smelled sweet and musky, but not quite like coffee. "The downstairs is a hookah bar," Joe said. "They close sometimes, though. This is the place to be if you need to stay up and study, or even just hang out when there's no other place to."

JD couldn't imagine staying up that late just to hang out. He'd done it to practice, and to write, but for that he needs silence and privacy, and this coffee shop was anything but that. They walked in, and the smell of coffee and cinnamon rushed into them. The place was well-lit, loud, and very busy. The music played over the bustling voices, and colorful paintings covered the walls and ceiling.

"It's pretty busy around this time, but I think I see an open booth," Joe said. "Go snag it, and I'll grab the drinks."

JD met Joe's urgency and walked briskly to the booth. The upholstery was very worn, but the table was clean. JD waited, looking around. Almost everyone looked like a college student, and most of them were working on laptops with textbooks open. One man sat at a booth alone strumming a guitar. The sound of the strings was indiscernible competing with the loudspeakers above them. JD suddenly felt overdressed. He took off his tuxedo jacket and laid it across his lap. As he unclipped his bowtie and buried it in his pocket, Joe returned with two large mugs, and a scone perched on the lip of one. He sat and passed the mug with the pastry to JD.

"Thanks," JD broke the scone in two and passed one half to Joe.

"Oh, no, I'm good. I'm actually on this intense runner's diet right now," Joe held up his mug. "Green tea," he said with a disappointed look on his face. "I got you the chai though. It's the best. Also, the grilled cheese here is to die for."

"Thanks again. I really should be the one buying," JD groaned.

"No, I insist." Joe took a sip. "So, what happened at this concert?"

JD grimaced and after a moment said, "I'm sure it went fine. I wouldn't know."

Joe cocked his head slightly.

"I didn't actually go… I left right before it started."

Joe's eyebrows shot up.

"Not my best idea…"

"Why didn't you want to go? Nerves?"

JD shook his head. It surprised him how much he didn't want to lie, even if it was to a stranger. "No…" JD took a sip. It really was a great chai. "Have you ever worked so hard at something, but somehow always fell short? I feel like all I do is practice, but…" he trailed off.

Joe waited.

"I mean. I'm good. And it's not like I don't like to practice. It's that the other French horn player is just better. And everything he writes is better. He had another solo tonight, and I just couldn't bear to hear it." JD thought about explaining the fight with Arjun but decided against it.

"I get that," Joe consoled.

"What sucks is that I love playing and writing music, but I can't get him out of my head. All I hear in what I compose is how mad I am that what he writes is better." The silence that followed was filled by a rock song playing from the speakers. "Sorry, I'm just—"

"No, it's okay." Joe said. "Is that why you said you're never going to play again?"

JD didn't say anything. It sounded like a dumb reason to quit something so important to him, but after all, it was a silly reason to miss a concert. The thought that JD got kicked out of his dream program because he was jealous of his own boyfriend made him want to puke.

"I really do get it," Joe said. "It's hard to care about something that much. I love to run, but in high school—" he took a sip, "in high school I was really self-conscious and way too hard on myself. I'm a great runner, and was back then too, but was just so stressed about getting faster. I fucked up pretty bad my senior year..."

JD didn't want to pry but wanted to know. "What happened?"

Joe continued. "I'm not proud of it. I doped for my last season of track. It was stupid and messed with my body really badly. The worst of it though, was that I got my relay team disqualified for state, and everyone at school knew why. I cared a lot about how everyone saw me after that, and I hated how my team saw me. And my coach. It was bad."

JD didn't know what to say. "I'm sorry," he managed.

"No, it's cool. It sucked, but I'm over it. My coach and I made up, and he's helping me train to get back into it. I'd love to join the collegiate team here, but it can be hard after something like that. I think my coach is going to vouch for me."

"That's great," JD said.

"Yeah, but I'm stuck with this for now," he gestured again to the green tea.

JD nodded. "I really hope you get on the team."

"Thanks, I hope you don't actually quit music."

JD thought about the email and swallowed down the embarrassment of it. He thought about his plea to the admissions office but couldn't help but feel like it was futile. Like it was just a formality she had to offer. He knew that it was ultimately Dr. Cleary's decision. There were dozens of waitlisted composition students, just at LU already. He couldn't blame her for wanting someone else. Someone who would show up to the concerts.

Joe smiled. "I can't believe you've never been here." He gestured around him at the bustling cafe. "It feels like a LU staple."

JD didn't want to confess that he'd rarely left campus at all his first year.

"My girlfriend, Haley, and I once spent the entire night here working on essays. We had this Composition class together the first semester of our freshman year, and we both procrastinated the last big assignment. It doesn't seem like the best place to study, but it chills out after 10 pm or so." Joe was looking around as if admiring the place. "We then went to that parking garage off Lake St., you know the one?"

JD nodded as if he did.

"We watched the sunrise from the top, even though it was like 20 degrees." Joe was smiling, mostly to himself. "It doesn't sound like fun, but it was."

"No, it does," JD affirmed. He wished he had a similar anecdote to add, but he didn't.

"I can't believe that was two years ago…"

"You're going into your third year?"

Joe nodded. "You?"

"I just finished my first."

"Nice, I wish I stayed over the summer after my first year. Are you in the dorms?"

"Yeah, Hansen Hall."

"Oh, no way! That's where I lived freshman year. I loved it. Most of my friends now were my hallmates—" Joe interrupted himself and cocked his head. Looking past JD with a confused look he said, "Wait, they're dressed like you. Do you know them?"

JD looked behind him to see Arjun and three of his friends, still in their tuxedos walking towards the counter. JD looked back at Joe; his face flushed with terror.

"Oh shit, is that him?" Joe asked.

JD's wide-eyed silence answered for him. He sank down into the booth. "Did he see me?" JD whispered.

The slight pity and amusement returned to Joe's eyes. "I don't think so."

A glimmer of relief showed on JD's face, but the panic still showed.

"Did you want to get out of here?" Joe asked. "We could probably sneak out while they order."

JD nodded. They left the half-drunk mugs and scone crumbs on the table, and JD followed Joe's lead towards the door. JD thought about looking over to see if Arjun noticed him but decided against it. The only thing worse than Arjun seeing him right now, would be for Arjun to know that JD saw him.

They swiftly made their way out the door and gingerly bounded down the wooden, creaky staircase.

Joe laughed when they exited the alley. "Well, that was exhilarating!"

JD chuckled weakly as the adrenaline faded. "Sorry to make us leave like that."

Joe shrugged. "I get it. Not the person you want to see right now. Besides, it was kind of fun. Felt like a spy movie or something!"

JD and Joe started walking down the street towards campus. The sun was lower in the sky, but still a bright, disarming white, and they squinted into it as they walked. JD wanted to find the situation funny, but really, he was just embarrassed. It was embarrassing that Arjun was JD's only friend, and everyone that they spent time with was really Arjun's friend, not his. They wouldn't come to JD to talk; they would go to Arjun. They would always take his side. It embarrassed JD that despite feeling like his world was falling apart, the only person he could think to tell was a stranger he'd just met. He pictured Arjun drinking coffee and telling all their friends what JD had done. JD knew what Arjun would tell them. What JD had really done. Guilt swelled in JD's chest, and confession bubbled up before he had another moment to swallow it down.

"That's not actually why I didn't go," JD stopped walking, "to the concert…"

The sun-scrunched smile on Joe's face twisted into concern. JD waited a moment before sitting on the curb of the sidewalk where they stood. Joe sat down next to him.

"We fought beforehand. He corrected me, and I stormed off. It's why I left, but I was going to go back in and play the show. I didn't. I just sat out there. The reason I didn't go back in…" JD paused for a moment, but Joe was silent. "That guy in there, the French horn player, he's actually my boyfriend. His name is Arjun, and I didn't want to hear him play that solo, that's true, but it's not really why I didn't go back in." The air around them was stagnant, and JD picked at the skin around his thumb, not looking at Joe. "One of the songs that we played tonight, the one with the solo, it's one of Arjun's favorites. It's his favorite solo. I remember he used to make me listen to the song with him on the bus—he's always loved it. I hate myself for wanting to have the solo instead of him, but he deserved it anyway. The worst part, though, is that there's this beautiful French horn harmony that plays behind the solo—that's me. That's what I was supposed to play tonight. It's a really big deal for a musician to play their favorite song or solo. To play it with a whole ensemble. For an audience. It doesn't happen often. And…" JD paused as the tears welled. "I left because I knew it wouldn't sound the same if I wasn't there. I knew that no matter how well Arjun played, it wouldn't sound right without the harmony."

JD let out the sob into his palms, and Joe rested his hand on JD's back, but didn't say anything. After a minute, JD looked up and said, "I knew it was a big deal to him, and that's why I did it."

"Shots (Broiler Remix)"
by Imagine Dragons

"I'm sorry man," Joe said after a while.

"Thanks. I just feel like a shitty person."

"I don't think you're a shitty person."

"Says the guy that just met me," JD said, "To the guy that just threw a French horn at him."

Joe laughed, "I mean it! Actually, my girlfriend and some friends and I are all hanging out tonight for the Fourth. Why don't you come along? We're going to the fireworks at City Park too; it should be a lot of fun."

JD smiled. "Thanks, but I should probably talk to Arjun tonight. We definitely have a lot to figure out."

Joe nodded. "Well, if your plans change, it's an open invite. But I get it; that's an important thing."

It pained JD to turn down the invitation. JD hated the thought of talking to Arjun; he knew he would have to apologize, but he also knew he'd have to tell him about getting kicked out. It infuriated JD to think that Arjun would be relieved or happy to find out that JD was no longer a Music major. But then JD thought maybe Arjun isn't like him. Maybe Arjun isn't jealous and petty. Maybe he doesn't wish ill on the person that he loves.

The two of them stood up from the curb. For a moment, it seemed to JD that they would say goodbye and start walking towards very different evenings. JD pictured himself thanking Joe for letting him ramble about his terrible day, and they would part, never having a reason to see each other again. JD also pictured himself going back to the dorms to eat dinner. He would either eat alone, or text Arjun and talk, and hopefully resolve what had happened well enough to eat together. The latter seemed impossible.

"Do you have dinner plans?" JD asked.

Joe smiled. "I'm meeting up with Haley actually, but I'm sure she'd love to meet you."

"Are you sure?"

"Oh yeah. The only thing she loves more than me is anyone new. I sometimes think she's too social. Where are you thinking?"

"I was just going to go to the dining hall, but we can go anywhere. You probably don't want campus food."

"You couldn't be more wrong there, my friend," Joe said.

"Wait really?"

"Oh yeah. Once you spend a year living on Top Ramen, a campus meal plan feels like gold. I really took the all-you-can-eat thing for granted."

"I could swipe you guys in? I've got tons of guest passes." JD couldn't tell if it was embarrassing to admit that he had no one to swipe in before now, but he pushed the thought away.

"Really? That would be awesome. Let me call her; I think she'll be super down."

While Joe made the call, JD stared down at his phone. He knew that he should text Arjun but couldn't get himself to do it. He decided to wait and do it in person. As guilty as he felt about the concert, he couldn't shake how mad he was still.

"She's in! She'll meet us there!"

The two walked towards campus, squinting into the low, early evening sun. As they walked, JD felt silly in his tuxedo. Normally, JD loved to wear it, but tonight he felt like an imposter—like some kind of wolf in sheep's clothing.

"You're going to love Haley," Joe said on the walk. "She's definitely going to try and peer pressure you to come out with us tonight, but you just gotta stand your ground."

JD nodded and hoped he wouldn't have to explain anything to her. He had confessed enough to one stranger tonight.

When they arrived at Hansen Hall, JD ran upstairs to change. He was relieved to be out of his tux, and even more relieved not to see Arjun or any other music students that were also staying in Hansen. JD put on jeans and a red tee-shirt and jogged back downstairs. By the time he got there, a girl was waiting with Joe.

She was shorter than Joe by about a foot, had a wild mess of curly red hair, and a mayhem of freckles across her cheeks. JD waved, and she lit up.

"You must be JD!" she said, practically bouncing over to hug him. Her energy caught JD off guard, and he didn't respond. "Thank you so much for swiping us in," she said, still holding on to him. "We haven't been back in like a year, and the pasta here is to die for." She pushed her wild hair behind her ears and said, "I'm surprised Joe made a friend on his own. He's so shy."

"I'm not shy, Haley, I'm just quiet." Joe retorted.

Haley looked at JD and shook her head, "Same thing." She turned and walked towards the entrance of the dining hall, leaving Joe and JD to follow her in.

When the three of them had gotten their food and sat down, JD was surprised by the amount of food on the table. Joe was very tall and very lanky, and Haley looked even more petite than she was sitting next to him, but they both had two towering plates of food. What was also surprising to JD was the contrast. While most of Joe's plates were raw vegetables, Haley had served herself two corn dogs, three chicken fingers, a slice of pizza and a plate full of fettuccine alfredo.

Haley noticed JD's eyes. "Hey, when you see a buck, you shoot it. Besides, Joe's whole health binge makes me look bad. Who actually eats that many vegetables? Like really."

"A lot of people, babe," Joe said, forking his salad.

"Ugh, this guy is always getting on me about 'fiber' and 'nutrients,'" Haley exaggerated the air quotes. "But I say you gotta live a little."

Joe smirked, rolling his eyes.

"So, tell me about yourself," Haley asked in between bites.

"Um," JD stammered. He'd always responded to this question with the fact that he plays the French horn and is a composer, but tonight it felt like a lie. "I just finished my first year."

"Oh cool," Haley said. "We just finished our second. I lived here my freshman year," Haley said. "This is where we met," she gestured to Joe. "One of my hallmates was actually Joe's friend from high school."

"Best friend," Joe interjected.

"Sorry, best friend. She introduced us and we've all been friends ever since."

JD nodded.

"We're all hanging out tonight for the Fourth. You should come," Haley said.

"Sorry, I can't tonight."

"No, you really should! It would be fun," Haley prodded.

Joe gave JD a knowing look and smirked.

"Sorry," JD insisted.

"Are you—"

"So how are you liking LU?" Joe interjected.

JD nodded, "I like it. Seems like a cool place."

"It really is," Joe said. "Have you been up to Horsetooth Ridge?"

JD cocked his head.

"It's those foothills just outside of town? It's a great place for hikes, but you can actually drive up to most of it. There's a really great view of the city from the ridge. We used to go all the time, but we haven't been in a while," Joe added.

"I feel like we've been there recently," Haley argued.

Joe shook his head.

"Hmm…" Haley said. "Anyway, it's really beautiful. What have you seen that you liked?"

JD was caught off guard by the question. Frankly, he hadn't seen much of town, or even campus. It seemed like he'd spent his entire freshman year in a practice room, or in his dorm, writing. He hadn't even been to the library. "Mostly just stuff on campus," JD managed to say.

"I really miss living on campus," Joe said.

"Really?" Haley asked.

"You don't? I loved the dorms. It always felt like there was something to do, and people to see. My favorite were the nights that we all would stay up all night, chug too much coffee, and stumble to class the next morning still jittery."

"I feel like you could do that now. Also, that sounds terrible," Haley said, moving on from an uneaten pizza crust to her bowl of pasta.

"What do you mean it sounds terrible? It was fun. I was telling JD about that night we stayed up to finish our Composition essays. When we watched the sunrise."

"Babe, that was awful," Haley said plainly.

"What do you mean?" Joe asked defensively.

"What do *you* mean? It was miserable. We were so sleep-deprived. I was grumpy all night. And the sunrise was so cold, it was the middle of December."

"I must remember it very differently."

"Hmm," Haley said.

Joe shrugged and took another bite of his salad. "I don't know. I feel like freshman year was kind of a magical time. Like we could do anything at any point. It was cool."

"Babe, like I said, you could do that now, why don't you?"

"I don't know. It's different. I feel like classes are more serious and stuff."

"I think you're romanticizing it a lot."

Joe shrugged.

JD didn't realize he was staring at his food until Haley and Joe stopped talking. JD looked up to see Arjun standing at the table, still in his tuxedo holding out an envelope for JD. JD took it and looked at Arjun. His face was hardened. "It's over, JD." Arjun said it indifferently and almost matter-of-factly, like he was answering a question about the weather.

"Wait, what?" JD managed to say.

"I don't want to talk about it. I don't think I have to explain why I'm hurt." Arjun's eyes were fixed at the wall behind JD. They looked to JD like polished black stones under a current.

"Can't we talk about it?" JD pleaded.

Arjun looked at him now. For a moment, JD expected himself to explode with anger. He expected himself to yell and fight, but when Arjun looked at him, all JD felt was guilt. He knew what the concert meant to Arjun. JD knew what he took away from him. Arjun walked away, leaving JD with only the envelope. He stared at it. Arjun had written him letters before, but each of them had been adorned with an elaborate, calligraphed "JD." Arjun had always said he loved JD's name, because capital letters were the most fun to write. The envelope in JD's hand was blank.

"Shot At The Night"
by The Killers

Joe and Haley looked at JD with wide eyes. Haley broke the silence, "Did he just break up with you?"

JD nodded slowly, still looking down at the letter. He could feel Joe and Haley's sad eyes on him. He looked up and tried to find Arjun but couldn't. Embarrassed once again, JD looked at Joe and said, "I guess my plans changed."

Joe managed a small fake laugh, but his eyes stayed the same. JD didn't know what else to say. For the first time, JD regretted meeting Joe and Haley. He hated that they saw what just happened. Even if they were practically strangers, JD hated the look on their faces. He replayed Arjun's words in his head; they made JD feel small, but he wished he was invisible. JD knew well how different those feelings were.

"Are you going to read it?" Joe asked.

"I don't know," JD responded.

After a moment, Haley spoke, "I have an idea!" She bounced up out of her chair and grabbed the letter off the table in front of JD.

"Wait!" JD protested.

"Haley, give the letter back," Joe said.

"Hold on. I don't think you should read it yet." She held the letter with two hands. "Not yet. I don't know what is going on, and you don't have to tell me, but I think reading this will ruin your night. I think you should wait."

"My night is already ruined. Can you just give it back?" JD pleaded.

Joe tried to reach for it, but Haley held it away from him.

"Hold on. I'll give it back if you promise not to read it tonight."

"Okay, fine," JD replied, exasperated.

"Also," Haley continued, "You have to come out with us."

"I think I'm just going to go to bed," JD said. "It's been a long, very terrible day."

"And that's exactly why you should come. If you sit in your dorm all night you will definitely read it. And if you come, you'll have fun, and you won't even think about the letter."

"C'mon, Haley, he doesn't have to," Joe said.

JD looked at Haley. Her light brown eyes stared back. "Besides, I have something that will make you feel better."

Part of him wanted to be alone, but the other part yearned for someone to talk to, even if it was two strangers. After a moment, JD said, "Fine."

"Okay, but you have to promise! No opening the letter, and you have to come along tonight." She held the letter up with one hand and the other out to shake. JD rolled his eyes and shook. She squealed and handed him the envelope.

JD took it and put it in his back pocket.

"I'm watching you!" she said. "No opening!" JD held his hands in the air in innocence. "Okay, cool. Let's get going. I've got something to help."

They all stood and cleared the table. As they left, all that JD wished he'd said to Arjun began to flood his brain. He wished he'd argued. He wished he stood up for himself and told Arjun how shitty he'd made him feel about himself all year. He wished he ripped up the letter in front of Arjun and told him to say what he wanted to say right there. What angered JD most was the finality of it all. That JD didn't even get a say in how it ended—it was just over. As they left the dining hall though, JD felt strangely relieved. He was relieved to have somewhere to go, wherever that was, and grateful to have something other than Arjun to think about.

Joe and JD followed Haley through campus into the large main plaza. She led them to the center wherein there lay a large wooden stump. It stood about one foot tall, three feet wide, and the concrete of the plaza was poured around its knotted roots. JD had seen it before, but never thought anything of it.

"What is this?" JD asked.

"It's The Stump," Haley replied simply.

JD waited for elaboration.

"You've never used it?" Haley asked, genuinely.

JD shook his head.

"I thought everyone knew about it."

"I'm at the music building off campus a lot," said JD.

"Oh, that makes sense. Well, the idea is that you stand on the stump and make a proclamation. It can really be anything, anything true, or what you believe to be true, but my favorite way to use it is to proclaim something that I love. Or all the things I love that I can think of. I yell them at the top of my lungs for everyone to hear, and something about it makes me feel better. You should try it."

JD and Joe gave her a confused look. JD couldn't help but feel like this wasn't something many people did; Haley's actions were bewildering, but her confidence was convincing.

"I'm serious. It will help! I'll go first." She stepped up to the stump and yelled loudly, "I love my friends! I love my mom! I love pasta! I love Diet Coke!" She beamed as the echo of her proclamation bounced off the buildings. "Oh, and my dog!" She hopped off the stump, "See? Easy."

JD and Joe looked around at the people walking in the plaza. It wasn't nearly as busy as it was in the fall, but people stopped to look at the girl yelling on a stump, and JD felt all their eyes. He went red in the face.

"I don't know—" Joe started.

"C'mon, it's fun and feels great!" Haley insisted. She pushed Joe onto the stump and looked at him excitedly. He stood there, face contorted. He put his hands on his knees for a moment as if winded, before inhaling, and bellowing, "I love to run!"

His echo carried even farther, and even more people stopped to look. Haley clapped for him as he dismounted. "Oh, and my hot girlfriend!" He pretended to yell. Haley laughed and they kissed.

"Alright, JD, you're up!" Haley said.

JD shook his head instinctively. "I don't think..."

"You'll love it! It's invigorating. It feels great to yell. Come on," Haley persisted. She grabbed his arm and pushed him onto the stump. JD was beet red and saw the faces of strangers already on him; some even stopped, expecting another crazy person to yell nonsense in the middle of the plaza. His mind raced, and even if he found it in him to yell at the top of his lungs, he didn't know what to say. He would have normally said 'music,' but the thought of yelling it tonight made him sick. He wanted to yell Arjun's name too, but that felt like a slap in the face to both of them now. After a few long moments, nothing came to his lips. His mind was blank, and he couldn't muster anything to say, much less yell or proclaim.

"You got this!" Haley said. The lack of worry on her face was contrasted by the look on Joe's. It was the same pitiful look JD had seen multiple times that evening already. JD shook his head and jumped off.

"Why don't—" Haley started.

"I just don't want to!" JD snapped.

There was a moment of awkwardness before Joe said, "That's fine. Let's get going! Dawn just texted and asked when we were heading over."

Haley's face lit back up. "Oh cool, yeah let's head over now! I can drive us."

"Midnight City"
by M83

JD sat in the back of Haley's small, white Ford Fusion. The music was loud, and the windows were down. The sun had begun to set into that brilliant, neon orange; the kind of color that seemed to pulse or sway, but just slightly—just enough to notice but not really see. JD rested his head on the open window and closed his eyes; he could still see the flashing of the light behind the trees as they drove, and he let himself feel the cool evening air and listen to the sounds that filled the car. JD admired the low rumble of the engine and the high-pitched sound of the wheels of the asphalt; the way the sounds mixed and muddled with the bright, electronic song was beautiful. It felt to him like a simple symphony, tiny and played only for them in the car. JD bathed in the sounds but couldn't ignore the sour feeling in his gut as thoughts about Dr. Cleary's email loomed; beautiful sounds and simple symphonies didn't seem to belong to him anymore. He wished that he could unread the email; he wished he could put it in an envelope and ignore it for the night too.

JD looked at Haley as she drove. He felt bad for snapping at her, but she seemed unperturbed. She had one hand on the steering wheel and danced slightly to the music. Her long auburn hair bobbed and swayed a moment behind the beat, and her many curly flyaways looked to JD like hot copper wire glowing in the lush orange light. She looked over her shoulder at JD, "I'm thinking we'll pregame a bit at our place, and then head over to the park for fireworks. Our friend Cody lives right by City Park, he's having a bunch of people over after."

JD nodded, "Sounds fun."

"You'll meet Dawn and Sara, my roommates when we get there."

"They're not just your roommates, Haley, they're like our closest friends. I've known Dawn for like six years," Joe interjected.

"I know, but they're also my roommates. They live there."

"Yeah, but…" Joe fumbled his words.

"Anyway, you'll meet the crew soon, JD. Better?" she looked smugly at Joe.

"Better," Joe turned and looked at JD. "I think you're really going to like them."

It was almost dark when they arrived at the house. The lawn was lush and overgrown, and there was a large cottonwood tree out front, full and heavy with its summer leaves. The streetlights hadn't turned on, and everything along the street was silhouetted by the dim evening glow. The lights were on in the house, and JD could tell that someone was home.

As they entered JD heard a loud, "Finally!" from a room down the hall. A girl walked in holding a wine bottle under her arm; the screw was already halfway in the cork. She twisted it twice and pulled it out the moment the door closed. "God, I thought you'd never get here."

"JD, this is Dawn, Dawn, JD," Haley said.

"Hello, let me get you all a glass. I've been carrying this thing around for hours waiting for you guys!"

"You didn't have to wait," Joe said to her as she walked into the kitchen.

"Oh, and drink this chardonnay *by myself?*"

"Also why were you carrying it around?" Haley added.

"So I could pop it the moment you got here. Now come on, let's party!"

They followed Dawn into the kitchen. The white, fluorescent overhead lighting made the kitchen feel small, and JD didn't quite know where to stand. He didn't want to come off as awkward as he felt. Dawn handed them all coffee mugs and started pouring. Dawn was tall, but still shorter than Joe.

She was wearing high-waisted, denim shorts, a black crop top, and large, clear-rimmed glasses but wore them on the top of her head nestled in her black, tightly coiled hair.

"Actually, I left my bike at the coffee shop, so I might have to go grab that. Also, Dawn, I'm not drinking tonight." Joe said, handing the cup back to her.

"Oh, I always forget. That damn diet of yours." Dawn replied.

Joe looked at Haley, "Babe, can you take me to my bike?"

"Of course, I can pick up some liquor for tonight too while we're out. We thinkin' vodka?" Dawn nodded, so JD did as well. "Cool, we'll pick that up."

"I didn't know you were twenty-one," JD said to Haley.

"I'm not, but Amber is!" Haley grinned and pulled out a driver's license with her face on it. "She's twenty-four actually. She's from Kentucky. She's also a Pisces, though, so take that as you will."

JD took the card and inspected it; he couldn't imagine himself walking into a liquor store and pretending to be old enough—rather, he couldn't imagine himself getting away with it.

"Yeah, a friend of mine from high school makes fakes. It's pretty good, honestly. Let me know if you want one," said Haley.

JD shook his head.

"Yeah, me neither," added Dawn. "I'm way too scared of getting caught. I'm glad you have one, though. Comes in handy."

"That it does! Alright, we'll be back soon. Don't drink all the wine before we get back," Haley said, grabbing her keys.

"No promises!" Dawn called out as they left.

A wave of panic came over JD. He had only met Joe a couple of hours ago, but his absence suddenly made JD feel out of place. He regretted not going with them. Being the third wheel in the getaway car of an illegal, underage alcohol transaction seemed to JD much more desirable than being the unwanted stranger in someone's house, but Dawn's bright, easygoing smile interrupted the thought.

"Alright, just you and me, JD. Hope you're thirsty." She consolidated all the wine into two mugs and handed one to JD. Dawn tapped her mug to JD's in a cheers and it made a dull clink. He took a sip and was surprised by the sourness. Dawn leaned against the linoleum countertop and smiled casually at JD. He wanted to say something, to fill the silence but couldn't think of anything. He felt strange initiating the small talk, but he also didn't want to bring attention to the fact that Joe, the one that invited him, wasn't there. Luckily, Dawn broke the silence.

"So, you're Joe's friend. Are you a runner too?"

"Oh, no. Not at all."

Dawn looked at him, prompting more.

"I actually met Joe tonight. We met at that coffee shop in the alleyway." A half-truth.

"Oh, the Alley Cat! I love that place. So, you go to LU?"

JD nodded. "You?"

"Yeah, what are you studying?"

"Music."

"Shut up. What do you play?"

"French horn and piano."

"Oh my god, the French horn is so beautiful!" Dawn took a sip from her mug. "I've been meaning to go to a concert. I think there's even a summer band, right?"

JD smiled. "There is. I'm in it. We had a concert today."

"How did it go?"

JD's stomach dropped, "Really good!" he lied.

"I can hear it in your voice; it did not go well! What happened?"

It surprised JD that he was talking about the concert. Normally, he was always trying to talk about music, but he expected himself to avoid the topic all night. JD thought about continuing to lie but didn't. JD gripped the mug full of wine in his hands and inhaled. "Well, can I be honest?"

"Please and always."

"I actually ditched the concert—"

Dawn looked wide-eyed at JD, "Wait, really? Oh my god, why?" She had a slight smirk as she said this. In a strange way, it comforted JD. It made him feel for a moment that the decision was just a rebellious story, not a life-ruining mistake. It felt good to gossip about his own life.

"Honestly, there's this other French horn player that is just way better than me. He sounds way better. Everything he writes is better. It's just exhausting."

"Ugh, that was my least favorite thing about being in a concert band."

"What is?"

"Just the competitiveness. First chair this. First part that. Playing test this. Solo that. Like, I found that environment exhausting too. It's hard to shake off."

JD nodded. He'd never thought about other people feeling that way. "I thought that was just me," he confessed.

"Oh God, no." Dawn scoffed. "Trumpet players are the worst, let me tell you." She took another sip. "And to try and write music in that environment? A shame. Honestly, I'm willing to bet this other guy's stuff wasn't even better than yours. It's probably all in your head."

"Well, I don't know about that," JD added.

"Tell me about your favorite piece you've ever written?" Dawn said, leaning in.

JD thought for a moment. "Well, the best song I think I've ever written was probably this piano piece I wrote a long time ago. It's got a pretty good—"

"I said your *favorite* piece. Not best." Dawn interjected.

JD took another sip and thought for a while. Dawn waited. "I think my favorite piece was probably one I wrote in high school."

"Tell me about it."

"It was a horn solo with piano accompaniment."

"No, tell me about it."

JD looked at her puzzled.

"About the song. How did it sound? What was it about?"

JD nodded. "It was a love song actually."

Dawn grinned.

"I wrote it for my boyfriend. At the time. I don't know… It was pretty. I played it for him, and his best friend played the piano accompaniment. He loved it a lot."

"You have to tell me more."

"I called it "Arjun's Prelude" because I'd promised to write him a hundred more songs." JD's openness surprised him, and his cheeks flushed.

"Oh wait, that is so sweet."

"Yeah, I never did though."

Dawn laughed. "I would love to hear it one day."

"I gave him the only copy of the song."

"I love that for him but hate it for me." Dawn said, taking another sip. "It sounds like you really love to write music."

"I love it, but I don't think I'm going to keep doing it." JD said. The sentence surprised him.

"Why?"

"I don't know. I used to think that I was going to compose beautiful symphonies or incredible scores for movies, but nothing that I've written lately is any good. I just don't know if I was meant to be the one that does all of those things."

Dawn didn't say anything.

"It's crazy too, because I've never really thought about doing anything else. It's always been a constant. When I played well, it was a good day. When I didn't, it was bad. Same for writing. Good composers write good songs; I haven't written anything good in a year… It's probably for the best that they kicked me out." JD mustered a smile at Dawn, but the casual easiness in the conversation had evaporated.

"Wait what?" Dawn asked.

JD regretted divulging everything he had.

"For ditching one concert?" Dawn clarified. "That seems excessive."

JD nodded.

"God, that sucks." The air around them held a tense sadness. JD wanted to say something or make a joke but couldn't find the words. He felt himself coming up with rationales for why he deserved it. For why it wasn't excessive. Or why it wasn't that bad; that someone else deserves it more, but the truth was that JD was devastated, and nothing he could say would change that. JD couldn't think of anything truthful that would make the conversation light and fun again.

Dawn seemed lost in thought before saying, "Honestly, fuck 'em."

"What?"

"Fuck 'em." Dawn took a long sip finishing her wine. "It sounds like they weren't helping you write better music anyway, who needs them? You love writing music; you should write music. Besides, you might end up writing better stuff without that other guy you hate being there."

JD thought about Arjun being described as 'the guy you hate.' JD had always thought of him as the person he loved, but at the same time, he didn't blame Dawn for thinking of it that way, considering how JD described everything to her. JD took a sip. "I don't know if it's that simple."

"Sure it is. If you love something, you should do it." Dawn poured herself more wine. She poured more into JD's glass. "You need this more than I do. What a day!" The air of nonchalance had returned, and JD was grateful.

Wait, so what do you play? You said you were in band?" JD asked.

"I used to play the trumpet."

"Oh, so you are the self-proclaimed worst? You said it yourself."

"No, I'm the self-proclaimed best. That's how it works as a trumpet player! But it was also the truth. Those other little buglers in high school couldn't hold a candle to me."

JD laughed.

"It's true! I would play circles around them." She took a sip. "I won't lie and say it's *not* in my nature to brag, but it definitely isn't in my nature to lie."

"So why don't you play anymore?"

Dawn's smirk faded, "Oh, just busy. Doing chemistry. To be a chemist. You know. And honestly, I don't really feel any desire to pick it back up. It doesn't inspire me the way it used to. It just feels like a thing of the past, you know?"

JD looked at her.

"I loved it, but" Dawn shrugged, "not my thing anymore."

"Well," JD took another sip and said, "If you love something, you should do it."

"Oh my god, rude. Touché, stranger."

JD heard the door open and Haley's voice call into the kitchen.

"Hey guys," Haley said as she walked into the kitchen. She set down a large plastic bottle of vodka onto the small wooden table. "Joe's biking. Is Sara here yet?"

"No," Dawn replied. "How'd it go at the liquor store? Successful, it would seem." Dawn picked up the bottle of vodka and inspected it.

"Super successful. Ed didn't even card me this time."

"He didn't card you?" Dawn's eyebrows shot up.

Haley shrugged as she poured herself a mug of wine. "Nope. I guess I've been going there for a long time now. Ed and I are on a first-name basis." She took a sip. "I guess Ed and Amber are on a first-name basis."

Dawn laughed.

"Maybe I should just become Amber full time," Haley mused. "Go to bars and live life as a twenty-four-year-old Kentuckian. Kentuckite?"

"You'd need an accent," Dawn added. "And you'd need to live life as a full time Pisces."

Haley recoiled, "Oh yeah, I forgot. Impossible."

JD observed the lightning-quick conversation in front of him. He had nothing to add, but even if he did, he had no idea when or how to fit it in. JD appreciated the light-heartedness in the air, but also somehow felt self-conscious in it. It reminded him of spending time with Arjun and his friends. Their friends liked to look at Arjun when they told stories or jokes. They wanted to know that he was listening or finding it interesting. JD liked being the one sitting next to Arjun and holding his hand, but JD couldn't help but feel like an observer in the conversation, as opposed to a participant.

Haley walked over to the bottle of wine sitting on the counter. She examined the amount and topped off her cup. "Okay, I'm gonna shower and change real quick," she said.

"Shower wine?" Dawn said, looking at Haley's mug, filled to the brim.

Haley smirked. "Not to be confused with a wine shower, which, as unpleasant as it sounds, I don't think is unwelcome."

Dawn laughed. "Okay, but be quick, because the moment Joe and Sara get here, I'm taking shots, with or without you."

"You wouldn't," Haley said.

Dawn shrugged coyly, "Maybe. Hurry then!"

Before walking away, Haley looked at the amount in JD's cup. She poured some of hers into JD's and said, "You need this more than I do. When I was going through a breakup, I was more of a red wine gal, but this'll do. Okay, be right back," Haley shuffled away, sipping and spilling as she walked.

JD went red in the face. He knew it wasn't really a secret, but he hated that Dawn knew about the breakup. He'd already confessed to getting kicked out of the music program; he didn't like Dawn knowing that he'd also gotten dumped earlier as well. JD felt a flash of anger towards Haley, but he held his tongue.

Dawn looked at him with a face that seemed to know how he felt. JD wondered if she might say something to console him, but instead shrugged and clinked her mug to JD's. It seemed to say, *'oh well, let's drink!* or *how weird, sorry about her!* Once again, JD was grateful for Dawn's proclivity for casualness.

"Work This Body"
by *WALK THE MOON*

A couple minutes later the door opened. "Hey!" Joe said.

"Hey Joe! We're in the kitchen," Dawn called out.

Joe entered, his helmet still on his head. He beamed at the sight of JD and Dawn.

"How was the ride?" Dawn asked.

"Divine. It is a beautiful night."

"*Divine*," Dawn mocked. "So do you want, like, chocolate milk or something? I guess we're out of wine already." She picked up the empty bottle and put it in the recycling bin.

"Some water will be fine, thanks. What have you guys been talking about?"

Dawn brought her shoulder to her chin, coyly. "Oh, you know, just the usual. I was just telling JD about all of your deepest darkest secrets, and then we mean-girl laughed about them together."

"Dawn, you can't joke about that." Joe said, seriously. "Firstly, I've heard your mean-girl laugh; it's very degrading. And secondly, you *do* know all of my deepest darkest secrets."

"My mean-girl laugh is not *degrading*, Joe. It's charming!"

Joe rolled his eyes.

"So how do you guys know each other?" JD asked.

"This is my best friend from high school that we talked about!" Joe said, pointing to Dawn.

"Oh, so you talked about me," Dawn squinted at Joe.

"All good things!" he said. "Yeah, we met on the first day of freshman year, actually," Joe said. "Sat right next to each other in Ms. Dennis's biology class."

"Yup. If only I'd known." Dawn said pensively. "I would have sat anywhere else," she jabbed.

Joe rolled his eyes again.

"Then we met the rest of the crew in our dorm freshman year of college." Dawn said to JD.

"We actually ate at Hansen Hall tonight," Joe said, "JD lives there."

"No way! I'm so jealous."

"Yeah, it was crazy being back there. Kinda miss it."

"JD," Dawn walked over to JD and grabbed both of his hands, "as one of my oldest and closest friends, I would be so honored if you would swipe me into the dining hall sometime very, very soon."

JD nodded, confusedly.

"Perfect, I can't wait. I've been living on Pizza Rolls for too long. Oh, I'm gonna eat so much soft serve ice cream." Then to Joe she said "So, JD said you guys met tonight? What's the story there? Spill."

"Yeah! I actually hit him with my bike," Joe lied, smiling.

"Wait, no way,"

"It was crazy."

"Are you okay?" Dawn asked JD.

"Yeah, I'm fine," JD said, going along with the lie. "He hit my French horn case more than he hit me. I got lucky."

Dawn squinted, looking at them both, "Someone's lying."

"Yeah, lucky for us, it padded the blow. It was crazy."

Before Dawn could ask another question or protest the lie, they heard the door open again. A girl with a long black ponytail walked into the kitchen holding a large cardboard box with two hands.

"Hi Sara!" Joe said.

"Hey." Sara said. She put the box down on the table and, noticing the stranger in the room, smiled at JD. "Hi, I'm Sara."

"I'm JD," he said, more timidly than he would have liked.

"I'm so glad you got off early and can pregame with us!" Joe said. "We're thinking about heading over to Cody's around 9ish."

"About that…" Sara started.

The excited look on Joe's face vanished.

She continued, "I don't know if I'm going to make it out tonight. I'm so exhausted."

"But it's the Fourth of July," Dawn protested. "Not that I'm celebrating, but I am trying to party! Are you sure?"

Sara nodded. "I'll probably turn in early." Sara's dark brown eyes smiled sympathetically at Dawn and Joe. "Besides, you guys know parties aren't really my thing."

"But—" Dawn tried to interject.

"I'll hang out with you guys while you pregame! Let me change really quick." She walked away before Dawn or Joe could say anything.

"Damn," Joe said. "I was really looking forward to getting her out tonight. I knew that she wouldn't meet us at Cody's, so I was glad she was gonna be here, but…"

"I was thinking the same thing," Dawn said.

"I think we could get Haley to help."

"Should we let it happen?"

Joe nodded, knowingly.

Moments later, Haley walked out with one towel around herself, and one towel wrapping her hair. "Hey D, can I borrow your red crop top?"

"Are you gonna wear it with those blue shorts with the white stars?" Dawn asked, with her eyebrows raised.

"Yes." Haley replied, sheepishly.

"Haley, we are partying, not celebrating!"

"But the color scheme is so cute!" Haley whined.

"You know what's not cute? War crimes, Haley!"

Haley pouted.

"Okay you can borrow it, but I get to be a bitch to you about it all night," Dawn concluded.

"I feel like you were gonna do that anyway," Haley crowed.

"You are so right. It's in the top drawer."

"Thank you!"

"Also, Sara's home, but she's not coming out." Joe added.

"What?!"

"I know. We're all bummed." Joe frowned.

'I'm on it." Haley turned around and marched towards Sara's room.

"Think she can do it?" Dawn asked Joe.

"Oh no doubt."

Dawn looked at JD, "Freshman year. It was the night before this crazy hard chemistry final that I hadn't studied for at all. Haley somehow convinced me to go to this weird poetry reading that she had to go to for class. It goes from six to nine thirty, mind you. Who reads poetry for that long? Anyway, peer pressure is a talent of hers."

"Although, I don't think convincing *you* to do something is that big of a feat," Joe said.

"It is when it comes to school. I was so sure I was going to stay home and study all night, but the next thing I knew I was high as a kite at some terrible poetry reading for three hours. *Three hours.* It was terrible. Yet memorable." Dawn smiled. "She's got a way of convincing anyone to do anything."

JD recalled how Haley had convinced him to come out. It reminded him of the letter in his pocket, which he'd somehow been able to ignore for a while. He tried to imagine what kind of deal or ultimatum Haley was making to get Sara to come out.

Within minutes, Haley walked back in with her make-up done and dressed in red, white and blue. She struck a pose as everyone turned to look at her.

"That was so fast?" Dawn said, bewildered.

"Years of practice," Haley batted her eyelashes. "How do I look?"

"I hate it, but you look hot," Dawn admitted.

"Thank you," Haley flipped her still damp hair.

"You look great, babe," Joe added.

"Also, I convinced Sara to come to the fireworks at least."

"No way! Great news!" Joe looked at JD knowingly.

Haley smiled. "Can we play some tunes? I can't take shots in silence."

Joe played a vibrant song from a portable speaker, and Sara entered the kitchen having changed into baggy jeans and a white t-shirt; she was nimbly tying off the end of a long French braid that started at the top of her head. She had dark, full eyebrows, high cheekbones, and a round nose with a septum piercing. When she finished with the braid, her brow smoothed into a soft, pleasant expression.

"It is officially shot o'clock," Dawn announced, "I'm going to pour us all a double, and if you guys don't take the full shot I'll be offended."

"Can you put some Sprite in the shot for me?" Haley pleaded.

"Absolutely not."

"It tastes so much better."

Joe joined in, "I don't know why you guys need chase, just drink it."

"So high and mighty about it, every time." Dawn rolled her eyes. "You're not even drinking."

"Yeah, also taking shots without chasing it is insane. Like, love yourself, babe," Haley added.

"It's not insane," Joe retorted. "It's like three seconds of burning and then it's gone. You like spicy food; it's the same thing!"

"It is not the same thing at all! Besides, you're one to talk, you can't even eat a jalapeño without crying," Haley said.

"Okay, bad example," Joe conceded.

JD witnessed the whirlwind banter in front of him and didn't have anything to add. For a moment he felt self-conscious again, like he was just a bystander looking in, but every time something funny happened and everyone laughed, Sara looked at JD too and smiled.

Dawn poured four shot glasses with vodka from the large plastic bottle that Haley brought. Joe filled an extra shot glass with water, and Sara calmly poured half of hers back into the bottle. JD wanted to admit that he'd never taken a shot, but the normalcy and routine of the moment prevented him. He'd seen it done. It would be fine.

"Oh!" Sara said "I almost forgot. I brought this from the club. It's my peace offering for not going to the party." She set down her shot and reached into the cardboard box to reveal two large mason jars. "It's lemonade from the kitchen! We made it tonight, but I snagged some on my way out."

Excitedly, each person poured themselves a glass. "Sara works at a country club, like, forty-five minutes away." Haley told JD.

"Yeah, I hate it, but the pay is good. And the perks." Sara added.

"This is such an excellent chase." Dawn said, holding the shot in one hand, and the lemonade in the other. "Thanks, Sara."

When everyone was ready, JD followed their lead in cheersing the shot, but when the glasses clinked in the air, no one moved. JD looked around, and noticed everyone was waiting and looking at each other, glasses suspended. JD held it there but stayed silent.

"I got it," Joe said. They looked at him and he said, "To cold beers, pressuring peers, and thinking of cheers."

JD clinked the glass and, one beat behind everyone, mirrored the motion of tapping it to the table before drinking. JD instantly regretted it. The artificial cherry ignited and made his whole mouth and nose catch fire. It tasted like gasoline. Half of the liquid found its way down his throat, but the other half found itself mid-choke, and spattered down JD's chin. The grimace on his face hid nothing.

"Oh no!" Haley exclaimed.

"We should have warned you. It's the worst quality vodka you can buy," Dawn added.

"Like, literally the bottom shelf," said Haley.

"No," JD coughed, "It's fine. Thank you."

"Lie," Dawn laughed. "Drink the lemonade, it helps a ton."

JD followed her instruction and was grateful for the sweet and lemony relief. After a moment JD asked, "Can I be honest?"

"Literally, always and please." Dawn repeated.

"That was actually my first shot."

Haley gasped. "No way!"

"Wait, that's what we should have cheersed to!" Joe said.

"Every time we take shots we try to come up with rhymes. We phrase them like toasts. It's kinda fun!" Haley told JD.

"Hold on," Joe started to pour everyone another shot.

"Another?" Haley said. "Don't mind if I do."

"That's actually a great idea." Dawn added. "We should probably get out of here within the next hour, and I don't want to be sober when I get to that party. I'm always fighting frat boys on the Fourth of July. I'll do it sober if I have to, but I'd rather not."

"You're a hero," Haley said, nodding.

"I'll take a water shot too, Joe," Sara said.

"She's a lightweight," Haley said to JD.

JD nodded and looked at Sara. She shrugged, unapologetically.

"Okay," Joe said, passing out the new shots. "What rhymes with JD?"

They held the glasses there again; JD was less anxious about the cheers and more about the small cup of poison in his hand.

"I've got it," Dawn cleared her throat. "To white wine, summertime, and JD's first time!"

JD followed the motions again but stared at the cup before drinking it. He noticed the others immediately drank the lemonade afterward, and he scolded himself for not doing that earlier. The lemonade helped immensely, but his face still showed the same displeasure.

"That was a good one," Joe said.

"Thanks, everyone." JD added.

"I think my first shot was with you guys," Sara said.

"It was!" Haley exclaimed. "It was in our dorm. That was one of the first times we all hung out."

"I still can't drink tequila," Sara said.

"Still?" Haley asked.

"Nope. Can't do whiskey either. Not since your birthday," she gestured towards Joe.

"That was so long ago," Joe cocked his head.

Sara shrugged.

"Dawn, I think our first shot was together, right?" Joe asked.

"Your first shot was with me, but mine was way later."

"Oh, that's right."

"Yeah, I was a real narc up until senior year," Dawn confessed.

"Not really," Joe added. "You were at the parties, you just acted drunk instead of drinking."

"I didn't act drunk, Joe, I'm just fun!" Dawn corrected.

"My first shot was at some shitty rich-kid's birthday party in high school." Haley said.

"Was that the one where that guy punched a hole in the wall?" Dawn asked.

"Oh my god, yeah. I forgot I told you about that. It was so gross."

"Memorable, though. Hey, Joe," Dawn said, "want to punch a wall out tonight? Make this night memorable for JD?"

"I would do a lot of things for you, JD, but that is not one of them."

"We could ask Cody to," Haley said. "He's a psycho."

As the banter about Cody continued, JD was grateful to have taken his first shot where he did. JD thought about the first time he drank with Arjun in his dorm. It was the first semester of college, and they drank a very dry, very cheap red wine from a box. JD hated the woody, bitter taste, but he loved the way it stained Arjun's lips the more he drank, and how it made his lips taste like sour fruit. JD pictured Arjun now and imagined him drinking with his friends talking about what JD had done. JD wanted to be angry about that, but part of him knew that Arjun deserved to be mad; Arjun deserved to drink with his friends and say whatever he wanted to say about JD.

The letter burned in JD's pocket. However upset the letter might make him, it would only hurt because whatever it said was true.

"Go"

by Donnie Trumpet and the Social Experiment

JD left to use the restroom. When he looked in the mirror, he noticed his flushed cheeks, and could feel the warm effect of the alcohol on them. He splashed cold water onto his face and dried it on a hand towel. He looked at himself again in the mirror and smiled. He didn't know why, but he felt the need to practice smiling casually. He wanted to make sure he looked okay as he smiled through conversations and said nothing. He laughed at himself and left the bathroom. As he walked back through the living room, he noticed a large, unlit neon OPEN sign hanging above the TV. He stopped and looked at it closer. It seemed odd to him to have one in a house. Dawn noticed him looking at it and walked over to him.

"That's our neon sign!" she said excitedly. "We found it in the garage when we moved in. It's real neon too."

JD nodded.

"We normally turn it on for parties and stuff," Dawn added, "but I don't see why we shouldn't have it on for the pregame." She reached behind it and flipped a switch. The sign flickered a moment, and then slowly came to life. They both took a step back. The red and blue glow was suddenly vivid and bright and casted a lavender hue over the whole living room. JD stared at it. The tubes themselves were almost white with intensity and hurt to look at directly, but the soft buzz it emitted was pleasant.

"We love it a lot." Dawn said. They stood there silently for a moment before she asked, "Do you feel kind of nostalgic when you look at it?"

JD furrowed his brow, "What do you mean?"

Dawn thought for a moment, "I don't know. These signs are all around. Some variation, of course, but I feel like we see these blue and red open signs all our lives. We all talked about it one night, and everyone had a specific memory that came to mind when they looked at it. Do you? Does anything come to mind? Like a memory?"

JD stared at it for another moment, but his mind was blank. He shook his head. "What does it remind you of?" he asked her.

Dawn looked back at the sign. The lavender glow settled onto her dark skin, and JD noticed the way the red and blue neon glistened occasionally in the reflective curves of her glasses still perched in her hair. "Something about the colors," she started, "or maybe it's the buzz, but it reminds me of being a teenager. My friends and I used to go to this corner store to buy sodas and snacks and sit outside on the curb. One night when we were like fifteen, my friend Lee tried to steal some cigarettes from the back. I was so mad because we went there all the time, but he snuck back and grabbed a pack. He was almost out the door with the cigs when Mr. Ken, the owner, caught him. He literally grabbed Lee by his shirt. I was scared shitless."

"What happened?" JD asked.

"When Mr. Ken realized who it was, he laughed. He put him down, opened the pack and handed one to Lee. He said, 'Take it. And if you actually like this shit, come back and we'll talk. But don't you ever steal from anyone.' Fifteen-year-old Lee, was of course whimpering like a baby by this point, but I was just so relieved." Dawn paused.

JD waited for her, but she seemed lost in thought and didn't continue. "Did he smoke it?" he prompted.

Dawn looked at JD and let out a laugh. "That's the funny part! We left and sat out in front of the store. We were all watching him, waiting for him to light it, and he looked at all of us and just ate it! I don't think I'd ever laughed harder."

The image made JD smile. He pictured the scene; he had no idea what Lee looked like, but the image of Dawn laughing in the light of the corner store's OPEN sign was easy to picture because it was in front of him.

"Lee was always like that though. Always causing trouble, but somehow never in trouble." Dawn trailed off and stared back at the sign. "I think he only ate it because he was afraid to smoke it. And he would hate to let us down—not give us a show." Her eyes softened into what looked like nostalgia or sadness, and JD thought about how sometimes the two are one in the same.

"Are you guys talking about the sign?" Haley interjected. "JD, what do you think about when you see it?"

He looked back at it and shrugged. Still nothing specific came to mind. The three of them sat on the sofa, still looking at the sign. JD thought about the story Dawn just told. He had no exciting story or adventure like it to tell. "What do you think about?" he asked Haley.

"It reminds me of this Thai restaurant that my family and I used to go to. We went like every weekend, and I would always get Pad Thai. My dad was always trying to get me to try other things, but I refused. I looked forward to that Pad Thai all week."

"Did it have a sign like this?"

"Honestly, I don't remember. It probably did, but either way, it's the memory that comes to mind."

Joe and Sara joined them. "I think of the sign at the roller-skating rink that I worked at in high school," Joe said. "We had one just like it, and I was in charge of turning it off at the end of the night. Not going to lie, it was sweet bliss turning that shit off every night. I worked way too much and way too late back then."

"He always turns this one off when we go to bed and lets out this big sigh of relief. It's so dramatic," Dawn said, rolling her eyes.

Joe smirked and shrugged at JD.

"What about you, Sara?" JD asked.

Sara took a sip of what looked like water and looked up at the sign. The white of her shirt seemed to glow in the light. She shrugged, "Well I grew up in Las Vegas, Nevada, so I can't help but to think about all the neon of the casinos and signs. My mom works at the Bellagio on the Strip, and we didn't live far, so I found myself driving through all of that often. Some signs are more interesting than others, but they all contribute."

"I would love that." Haley said. "I think that would be so beautiful to see every night."

"Except that you can't see the stars," Sara retorted.

"Honestly, fuck the stars. They aren't that bright, and they just kind of hang there and do nothing." Haley said, sipping her drink nonchalantly. Dawn busted up laughing, but Sara and Joe looked almost offended.

"Babe! That feels so blasphemous!" Joe said, horrified.

"I mean, they're great, but compared to beautiful, glowing neon signs, especially in Vegas? They just seem kind of boring."

Haley jabbed with a shrug. Her grin showed her pleasure in causing the stir.

"But they're not real, you know? How do you not like the stars?" Joe protested.

"It's not that I don't like them, I'd just rather look at something brighter, closer, and more interesting. Besides, neon signs are *real*. There's one right behind you." Haley said.

"I mean that they're man-made," Joe corrected. "The stars are whole suns—enormous celestial bodies—trillions of miles away. How is that not more interesting?

"But they're just so tiny in the sky. And they don't really do anything," Haley said.

Joe closed his eyes in exasperation and defeat. "Unbelievable."

"I'm with you Joe." Sara soothed.

"Me too," Dawn added, "although I love the hot take, Haley."

Haley beamed. "Anyway," she said, turning to JD, "about the sign. Did anything come to mind?"

JD looked up at the neon, but again thought of nothing. He wanted to say something to fill the silence, but he couldn't even come up with a lie. Part of him felt silly for being self-conscious for not being able to think of something—anything, but another part of JD really wanted to participate. He didn't want to feel like a bystander, and he didn't want to lie. His silence hung heavy in the air. The buzz of the neon seemed to mock him.

Joe jumped in, "Didn't you guys have some song you associate with the sign?"

"Ooh, yeah, the neon song!" Haley lit up. "Dawn we should show JD the song!"

"Oh no, it's so stonery." Dawn said, cringing.

"No, I feel like he'll like it. He's a music person." Haley stood up excitedly and retrieved the speakers from the other room.

Dawn turned to JD, "Okay, forewarning, we were stoned out of our gourds at the time—"

"And we found this song that sounds like what neon looks like," Haley interrupted.

JD squinted in confusion.

"Trust me, it's cool," Haley reassured. JD was grateful for the subject change away from what he couldn't think of or hadn't experienced, but it still stung that he didn't contribute.

"It's a great song," Dawn said. "The instrumentals have such a…" she hesitated, finding the word, "fluorescence to them? It's bright and fun, but still such a nighttime song. I don't know, I think I'm making it sound dumb. You should just play it."

"Give me a second," Haley scrolled through her phone. "Found it! Okay, listen."

She put the speakers up by the sign. The song that played was groovy, brassy, and electronic. JD didn't understand where she was coming from with the song sounding like neon, but as he listened, he looked around and saw the group, bobbing and swaying, bathed in the purple glow; Dawn had her eyes closed and sang softly along. Sara lay on the ground and tapped her feet, alternating to the beat. Joe had his arm around Haley and was thoughtlessly beaming. JD wanted to take a picture but didn't. He wanted to capture the moment somehow, but he knew that a picture would only show a small part. It would show their facial expressions, and it would show the blue and red light bouncing off the walls and mixing in the air. But it would be missing the song. JD thought about it and couldn't help but feel like the picture would be missing the brassy fluorescence that Dawn talked about. It would be missing the soft buzz of the sign, harmonizing with the tune. JD conceded that what the picture would be missing wouldn't be the way that neon looks, but the way it sounds.

When it ended, Haley looked eagerly at JD, "Well?" she said. Everyone turned to JD waiting for an opinion, a critique, or perhaps more questions about what was clearly a display of something very unique to the group. JD thought for a moment about what to say. He wanted to agree or share his approval of the song but couldn't find the right words. There was a moment when he thought someone would again fill the silence, but they waited. JD looked at the sign and said, "I actually think something came to me—the memory when I look at the sign."

"Oh?" Haley prodded.

JD smiled, "It reminds me of the night that I took my first shot."

Joe beamed again.

"I love that," Haley added. "Wasn't that the night Joe punched a hole in the wall?"

"Not gonna happen!" he responded.

"How are we doing on time?" Dawn asked, suddenly.

Joe looked at his phone and nodded. "We're doing fine, why?"

Dawn was looking at the sign and pushed her lips to the side in thought before she said, "Can I show you guys something?"

Interlude:
"The Firebird Suite: The Final Hymn"
by Igor Stravinsky

They followed Dawn into her room. The room was slightly cluttered with clothes on the floor, but the bed was made. The room was lit only by a floor lamp with a colorful lampshade near her bed, and the walls were empty save for one giant "poster" on the wall across from the door. It was random newspaper pages taped together to the wall with a single quote painted in purple across it. It read: *Per aspera. Ad astra.*

Dawn reached into her closet and pulled out a leather case. She set it on the ground and opened it.

"Are you going to play?" Joe asked, almost hesitantly.

"Yeah. Actually, can you go grab that vodka? I'm gonna need a swig." Joe bounded out the door and within seconds returned with the plastic bottle. Dawn took a quick drink from the bottle and let out a quick exhale. She said, "Alright, we should probably get going soon, but let's try this out."

She waited a moment before pulling out the silver trumpet. JD could tell it wasn't new, but it was well taken care of. She held it in her hands and pressed the valves down. "Oh yikes," she said as they resisted. She opened them up and generously applied the oil she had in the case. She worked the valves slowly massaging them until they started to give. Everyone was silent, watching her. "Alright, old man. Let's see if we still got it," Dawn held the instrument up to her lips. She closed her eyes and inhaled deeply. She blew a couple of spits finding the placement on her mouth and then jumped notes and climbed up and down scales, warming up, until she stopped on a single note. Her brow was furrowed, her mind buried in the sound. JD recognized the note immediately as the concert pitch. Nostalgia and excitement ran through him as he thought about all the times he'd heard the note played before a performance; a single note demanding the attention of an auditorium. Dawn's silver trumpet did the same, echoing on the walls of the small, dimly lit bedroom.

"Alright, no judgment," Dawn said, interrupting her own note. No one said anything, and everything was still. The sound that followed the silence was a warm whisper that felt like it came from the floor rather than the trumpet. The sound grew, and the tune developed slowly behind the notes, sounding big and noble, but played tenderly, almost delicately. Every note swelled and felt heavy in the small room, as if each note was being pushed and pulled through water. JD recognized the song. It was the finale to a Stravinsky ballet. The part that Dawn played was written for the French horn, and JD had always loved it. Dawn played it on the trumpet, but so carefully that she mellowed out and rounded out the brassy sharpness that JD expected from a trumpet. JD closed his eyes and it almost sounded like a French horn resounding in a concert hall.

No one said a word or looked at anything but the white glint on the instrument, and Dawn's furrowed concentration. The song began to build. The melody stayed the same, but each note grew and took up more space in the room. When the tempo picked up, Dawn played the trumpet to its brightest, boldest sound. The soft, humble tune grew and began to run into something dramatic and powerful. It became the kind of finale that invited a curtain to fall and an audience to stand in uproar. What amazed JD the most was how the song seemed to be two beautiful things at once: it was equal parts tender ballad and epic finale; it was a gentle hymn and a battle march all at the same time. When Dawn played the last note, it seemed to echo in the room and down the hall. JD was awestruck.

With her eyes still closed, Dawn brought the instrument down from her lips and into her lap. She lowered her head into a position that looked to JD like a prayer, but the group began to clap, interpreting it as a bow. She chuckled slightly, and when she looked up at everyone, JD noticed that her eyes were blurry with tears.

"How did it feel?" Joe asked.

Dawn put the trumpet into its case. She smiled at him and said,

"Kind of like seeing an old friend."

Joe nodded.

JD wanted to say something. He wanted to say that it was the best rendition of the song he'd ever heard. He wanted to say that she was an incredible trumpet player. He wanted to ask if she'd ever gotten the chance to play it in concert, but that thought suddenly put a pit in his stomach. It reminded him of Arjun and the concert JD had just ruined for him. He pictured Dawn finally getting to play this song in concert, and someone she trusted ruining that once-in-a-lifetime opportunity. He had just met Dawn, but the thought of doing what he'd done at the concert to her made him want to cry. He pushed the thought aside, but it was too late. He hated himself for souring this moment in his mind. He had truly loved Dawn's performance. JD still wanted to say something, but he didn't.

Dawn cleared her throat, "Alright. We should get going; I don't want to miss the fireworks."

"National Anthem"
by Lana Del Rey

"Are you sure you want to bring that? We can just pitch at Cody's," Joe asked Haley as she put the handle of vodka into her large purse.

"I'm gonna take pulls during the fireworks," Haley said, matter-of-factly. "I'm trying to be my perfect drunk by the time we get to the party."

Joe nodded and smirked. "Alright, let's load up."

They all followed him out and into Haley's small white car. Dawn, Sara, and JD sat in the back; it was a tight squeeze, but the excitement in the air made the closeness more welcome.

"Alright, Dawn, do you mind playing some tunes," Haley asked, passing her the cord. "I'm sure you will think of a Fourth of July bop faster than I can."

Dawn took it, pursing her lips. "Honestly, all that comes to mind is the National Anthem, but there's no way I'm playing that." She thought for a moment, "and Katy Perry's 'Firework,' but again, I don't think that's the vibe."

"Honestly, I love that song," Joe said.

"That's why you don't have the aux cord," Dawn quipped.

"Ouch."

"I'm with you, Joe," Sara said.

"Thank you, Sara."

"Ooh, I got it! You know 'National Anthem' by Lana?" Dawn said, mostly to Haley.

"Yeah, play it," she responded.

"You'll play Lana del Rey, but not Katy Perry? What's the difference, really?"

Dawn scowled at Joe in the rearview mirror. "On one hand I'm mad that you said that, but on the other I don't have a rebuttal, so I'm going to ignore it."

Joe laughed.

"This one isn't my favorite of hers, but it does have this really cool part in the beginning that is definitely relevant. It's this beautiful string line, and then fireworks sounds play over it, listen."

They obeyed and listened closely. The violin melody that played was bright and nostalgic. Dawn closed her eyes, and JD watched as she followed the notes with her fingers. It wasn't as if she was miming the notes on an instrument, but rather that just the tips of her fingers were dancing and finding the beat.

The firecracker sounds started, and Dawn smiled wide. JD closed his own eyes. He heard what she heard: beautiful sounds, but he didn't smile.

He listened as the music and strings mixed and bounced off the crackling and echoing pops. It reminded him of the moment in the car earlier that evening, when the notes of the song mixed with the sounds of the car engine and tires on the road. Something about music finding its setting; it was the kind of beautiful that put a heavy stone in JD's chest. He felt a deep longing and wanted just to be a part of it—to be someone making and writing beautiful sounds.

Unfortunately, it was the kind of song JD would have wanted to show Arjun. JD remembered when they first met in high school. Before they even dated, they would send each other songs to listen to; they would talk about music for hours. In college, JD stopped showing Arjun the songs he loved. JD had felt so uninspired for so long, and he was self-conscious about everything he wrote. He stopped sharing with Arjun the songs he wrote and even the songs he liked. Music in general had become hard to talk about; it felt like some kind of wound that opening up to Arjun just made worse. JD had rationalized that Arjun was busy writing beautiful music anyway. He didn't have time to worry about JD's writer's block, and he didn't need to listen to the songs that inspired JD. Looking back on all of it,

JD felt stupid for how jealous and petty it all seemed to him now.

The song continued and Dawn said, "There's something about the strings and the fireworks that's just so… sensory. I love it."

JD knew exactly what she meant. There was something so cinematic about the strings and fireworks. It was the kind of music that was easy to picture in your mind; it was easy to feel surrounded by it. JD opened his mouth to speak, but again didn't say anything.

Dawn played Katy Perry's "Firework" after, and Joe sang loudly and with a kind of melodrama that made everyone laugh. Dawn and Haley joined him, and the loudness shooed away JD's thoughts about Arjun. They pulled up to the park and Joe finished his concert.

"Okay, you were right, Joe. I guess it was the vibe." Dawn said, stepping out of the car.

"You're welcome!" Joe said, smugly.

"Your singing, however?" she jabbed.

"I never claimed to be a good singer! I am who I am," Joe shrugged.

"Honestly, I respect that a lot," Dawn nodded.

"Do you guys know where they are?" Haley asked, looking at her phone.

"No, let me call Cody. I think he and his roommates are already here," Joe said. City Park was crowded and dark, but the group was flagged down by someone in a red tank top, a wide brim straw hat, sunglasses, and a beer in his hand. JD couldn't imagine why he was wearing the hat and glasses in the dark, but as he got closer, he realized that he recognized him. Their friend, Cody, was Cody Nguyen. The best percussionist at LU. He'd been lead percussionist in the high symphony for three years— even as a freshman. No one does that. Their friend was *the* Cody Nguyen.

Haley and Joe had mentioned Cody but didn't mention that he was also in the music program. JD had met him before, but he doubted that he'd recognize him. Cody was always surrounded by people in the music building. Whether they were friends, or just people trying to get him to join their ensembles, JD never knew.

"Hey!" Cody called out. When they reached him, he hugged everyone. He saw JD and took off his sunglasses with a perplexed look. "Hey, JD! I didn't know you knew these guys?"

JD was caught off guard by the fact that he didn't have to introduce himself. He stammered, and Joe stepped in, "Wait you guys know each other?"

"Yeah, we're in the same program," Cody replied. "Aren't you in the summer band? How'd the concert go?" he asked JD.

JD's stomach dropped and he lied, "It went great!" There was no way that Cody wouldn't find out sooner or later that JD was no longer even in the program with him. JD tried not to think about it.

"Hell yeah," Cody said, handing out beers.

"I always forget you have this double life as a classical musician. You never talk about it." Joe said to Cody.

Cody shrugged.

"You should invite us to a concert," Haley demanded.

Cody shrugged again, "It's really no big deal. It's just for class."

JD was surprised by his nonchalance. He knew Cody took music seriously; he had to. JD couldn't imagine himself saying that a concert was no big deal. Even if he had just ditched one himself. It was still a big deal.

"Besides," he continued, "you'd have to see me in a hoity toity monkey suit. That's Business Cody. He doesn't smile and plays the wind chime. Weekend Cody is drunk and plays the drums. He's way more fun."

Haley laughed, "Well, all the more reason. JD, have you seen him play?"

JD nodded. "Yeah, I actually went to his semester recital in May. He's really good."

"I saw you in the audience," Cody said. "I didn't get the chance to thank you after."

JD recalled the recital and felt slightly embarrassed. Cody's recital was one of the few that filled up the auditorium, but Arjun didn't go, so JD sat by himself in the back. He remembered feeling invisible back there, observing the recital as well as the crowd watching it. What JD remembered most about it was the applause at the end.

JD also thought about "Business Cody." It wasn't true that he never smiled. Cody was like Arjun in the way they both lit up the room without even knowing it. JD always noticed the way people acted when Arjun was around. Whether or not they said anything, JD could tell that they were excited Arjun was there. Cody was the same way. It surprised JD that Cody noticed him at his recital. JD was never the type of person people noticed when he walked into a room.

The thought was interrupted by Haley's voice, "Oh my god, Cody, did you just hand me an IPA?" Haley winced and held the bottle at an arm's length.

Cody laughed, "I did, and you live in Colorado, Hales. You've got to get used to it."

"I most certainly do not," Haley retorted.

"You turn 21 in a couple months, and we are going to go to breweries," Cody explained. "And they aren't going to have PBR or Natty Lights."

"First of all," Haley said matter-of-factly, "Natty Light tastes like shit, and PBR is delicious. And second of all, not every beer at a brewery is going to taste like grass."

Cody opened his mouth to respond, but he was interrupted by a bright flash of red followed closely by a booming snap. Everyone's heads whipped to the sound, and the park erupted in cheers. Everyone sat, and JD took a seat on the blanket next to Sara. They all stared with their necks craned up as the show continued. There were explosions of every color, and it was beautiful, but what struck JD most was the sound. He noticed how the booms and crackles seemed to take up all the space in the night sky; it seemed like the fireworks' desperate plea to be noticed by the universe, only to disappear within seconds. They left behind only smoke, clouding the silent stars behind them. JD tried to see the stars from behind the smoke but couldn't help but admire the dramatic performance right in front of him.

He closed his eyes and felt the sounds in the air around him; it reminded him of the intro to the song they'd listened to earlier. He tried to imagine an orchestra of strings playing along with the fanfare of explosions, but as he soaked in the beautiful sounds, a painful ache settled in. JD wished he was watching the scene with Arjun. He pictured Arjun, wide-eyed, grinning, and taking in every spark and glimmer. He imagined all the things Arjun might say to JD as they watched together. He pictured Arjun telling JD about what chemicals make each color, or telling a story about how his mother had always hated fireworks, or reminding JD of the New Year's Eve they spent together senior year, and how cool the sparklers looked in the pictures they'd taken. JD let his mind wander in the warm, sweet fantasy, but his gut pulled him back to reality; the letter in his back pocket burned. He knew at that moment that it was time to read it. Whatever the letter had to say, he was ready to hear it.

JD looked around. Everyone was wide-eyed enjoying the fireworks. Haley reacted to each one as if surprised that they kept coming, and Joe was laying down with his head in her lap. Dawn sat with her knees pulled into her chest staring up, wordlessly; JD noticed that she had moved her glasses from the top of her head and put them on. JD was confident that no one would notice him reading the letter, and he rationalized that as long as it wasn't Joe or Haley, they wouldn't care.

He pulled it out of his back pocket. He knew he'd miss the show and would have to steal the light of the flashes to read each sentence, but JD couldn't wait. JD knew that the letter would be hard to read. He knew that he'd hurt Arjun, and that Arjun would have every right to list the ways, but JD hoped, in that moment, that the letter would have some ounce of hope that things might not be over, at least not for forever. It felt impossible to think that loving someone could be a temporary thing—that all this time with Arjun was just over in a single night. JD thought about the feeling he had when Dawn played her trumpet. It seemed unforgivable what he did to Arjun, but he knew that he needed to apologize—to text Arjun, or maybe write him a letter back—but before he did, JD knew that he'd have to read the letter and hear what Arjun had to say.

JD still wished that his name was on the envelope, but as he opened it, he noticed that it wasn't sealed either. Arjun had tucked the flap into itself, as if touching the letter to his lips would burn him. JD swallowed down the shame and let the next bright flash illuminate the letter.

Except that it wasn't a letter. JD held the worn, tattered paper in between his fingers. Each firecracker seemed to mock him as it made the title visible. In front of him, was his own handwriting: "Prelude for Arjun" and the perfectly inked music notes blotting the lines across the page. He noticed the new creases folding the page into thirds for the envelope and the deep worn creases where the song had been folded into eighths and kept in a wallet. The sight of it made JD want to cry; he wanted to scream and rip the song apart; he wanted to have never written it for him in the first place. JD checked the envelope for anything else—any kind of note, but it was empty. The message was clearer than any letter could have been. Arjun had wanted to get rid of the song; he wanted JD to know that he'd never want to hear the song ever again. There was nothing to write back. There was nothing to say. Without thinking, JD tore the song apart, and stuffed the pieces into his pocket.

JD looked up, and everyone was engulfed by the show. Everyone except Sara, who looked at him, scooted closer, and continued to watch the show with her shoulder up against his. JD didn't want to cry, but he let out silently what he couldn't hold in, and watched the beautiful lights make beautiful sounds.

"My Body"
by Young the Giant

The fireworks show ended with a spectacular fanfare. JD looked at Haley and thought that the sheer joy she seemed to feel might kill her. For some reason it annoyed JD. When it ended, Haley employed the group in an excited discussion of the show. Quietly, Sara turned to JD, "You okay?"

JD tried not to show it on his face, but he was seething. He was filled with a painfully familiar feeling and knew that it was jealousy. He hated the thought that Arjun would show up to rehearsal on Monday like nothing happened. JD hated the thought that all of Arjun's friends would wordlessly avoid JD. Arjun would continue to write beautiful music, and JD wouldn't. It was the most jealous JD had ever felt, and it embarrassed him how familiar he was with the feeling.

JD nodded in response to Sara and gave her a half-hearted smile.

"Do you want to talk about it?" she asked.

JD's eyes were still puffy, and his nose was red from wiping it on his sleeve. He shook his head, "No, but thanks. Haley told me not to read it tonight. She was right. Don't tell her I read it."

Sara nodded. "Well, I'm probably going to head out soon if you want to come." She looked up to make sure that everyone was still distracted by the conversation led by Haley and now Joe. "It's about an hour walk, but not too bad."

JD thought for a moment. Haley was right: what was in the envelope did ruin his night. He wanted to go home and mope, but he also wanted to go home and plan exactly what he would say on Monday in the meeting at the admissions office. He felt the urge to say whatever he needed to say to get back in. He felt the urge to compose something that night—something so good that they'd have to let him back in. He'd avoided it long enough. "Yeah, I'll head back with you."

Before anyone stood up, Joe's voice addressed the group, "Okay, I have to get everyone else in on this." He said this loud enough to get JD and Sara's attention. They turned to him. "Haley here has a lot of shit to say about the stars."

"Okay," Haley said. "Since you want to get into it, all I said is that these fireworks are much brighter and more impressive than the stars."

"And I'm trying to say that the stars are giant, burning celestial bodies lightyears away in every direction, and that is much more impressive."

"But they're so far away. They just kind of twinkle. If we're talking wow-factor—if we're talkin' razzle dazzle, the fireworks take the cake." Haley said this matter-of-factly, and Joe put his face into his hands.

"They had this debate earlier about the stars and our neon sign," Dawn explained to Cody and his roommates.

"Guys, tell me I'm not crazy," Joe pleaded.

"I'm not saying you're crazy, I'm just saying you're wrong," Haley said.

"Wait, so what's the debate here?" Cody asked.

"I think it's: Which is better, the stars or man-made sources of light." Dawn said this with a questioning tone.

"I wouldn't say better," Haley added. "I think it's more: Which is more exciting or awe-inspiring? I get that the stars are these big, important things, but they're so far away. They're tiny. You saw this fireworks display; it was incredible. It was bright, and you could feel it."

"How do you not find the stars awe-inspiring?" Joe asked.

"I wouldn't say that I don't, but I don't see you marvel and gawk every night when you walk outside."

Joe rolled his eyes, "Help me out crew."

"I don't know. I'm staying out of this one," Cody said with his hands in the air.

"Me too," Sara added.

"Dawn?" Joe prompted.

"You know, I was pretty far on your side earlier, but Haley is making some great points."

"Oh, come on. It's the stars!" He pointed up and everyone looked to see the smoky haze clouding his point.

Haley squeaked, holding in laughter. He scowled at her and said, "That's it. We're heading up to Horsetooth tonight. After the party, I'm driving everyone up, and you are going to be *awestruck*!" A sheepish grin broke through as he said this.

"I'm in. We'll put it to a vote at the end of the night. Loser buys the drunk pizza," Haley proposed.

"You are so on," Joe grabbed her hand and shook it.

It was hard for JD to care about the debate between Haley and Joe. He couldn't help but feel like Haley was just trying to get a rise out of Joe, and all JD wanted to do was go home and prove that he also belonged in the music program. That all the work he'd put in wasn't a waste, but as he thought about it all, an entirely new feeling began to grow. JD thought again about the song Arjun had given back. He didn't write anything to JD, but the message was clear. By giving back the song, Arjun seemed to say, *It's over forever. I never want to see you or think about you ever again.* To JD, the breakup had a new varnish of permanence to it that he hadn't felt earlier that night; Arjun wanted nothing to do with JD. JD thought about walking into rehearsal after somehow pleading and begging hard enough. He wouldn't have Arjun welcome him back. At best, Arjun would politely ignore JD, but he would have every right to wish JD had never gotten back in. The hopeless feeling sank deeper into his stomach.

"There's no way you win this, Haley." Joe said confidently.

"About that..." Sara interjected.

"Oh no," Joe said.

"You might have to put my vote in for Joe now. I'm heading home." Sara said this carefully, as if expecting the disagreement that followed.

"Noooo," Haley groaned dramatically. "You can't leave, we need your vote later!"

Sara smiled but shook her head. "Yeah, no. JD and I are heading back now."

Haley leered at JD. "You have to stay! I need your vote too. You're my swing state vote for the landslide win at the last minute!"

JD expected Joe to laugh at that, but when he looked at him, Joe was deflated.

Sara spoke, "We'll have to put our votes in now. And honestly Haley, I think both our votes are against you."

"Yeah, right now they're for Joe," Haley complained. "That's why you guys need to stay."

Sara shook her head again, but Joe broke in, "You guys should stay. It'll be a lot of fun." The look on his face reminded JD of when Joe first invited him to get coffee earlier that day. It made JD think twice about leaving. JD looked at Sara and could tell that she had a similar hesitation. They'd prepared to resist Haley's peer pressure, but Joe's seemed to carry a different weight.

Cody broke in, "Yeah, stay for just a bit. I've got a surprise for you guys back home."

Haley lit up, "See! You have to stay!"

JD thought for a moment. He wanted to get back home, but an idea crossed his mind that he couldn't ignore. It occurred to him that Cody could be his ticket back into the program. Cody Nguyen was the music program's golden boy. Dr. Cleary boasted about him every time a percussion instrument came up in conversation. JD wondered if Cody talked to Dr. Cleary on his behalf, it would help him get back into the program. The chances were slim, but the thought of Cody Nguyen advocating for him made JD feel so hopeful he almost felt excited. Cody hardly knew JD, but JD knew that any chance he had to get back in, he had to take.

Sara looked at JD and something about the look on his face must have told her that he wanted to stay. "Okay, I'll stay for a bit," she said.

"Yay!" Haley said, "JD?"

He nodded and she squealed.

"Alright let's head back, looks like the crowd has thinned out." Cody said.

"What's the surprise, Cody?" Dawn asked, standing and putting her glasses back into her tight curls.

"And ruin the surprise? Obviously, I'm not going to tell you."

"Worth a try," Dawn shrugged.

They all started walking across the park. JD hung back and walked with Sara. "Hope it's okay that we're staying. I don't want to mess up your plans," JD said.

"Oh, I didn't have plans. I was just going to go to bed."

JD nodded, "That doesn't sound bad. I feel like parties aren't my thing, but there's a first time for everything!" JD realized the confession he'd made after he said it.

"Wait, you've never been to a party?" she asked.

His face flooded and confirmed the truth.

"Oh, no shame at all! I guess it makes sense—wait, no I don't mean—I mean because of your first shot. Sorry," she stammered.

"No, it's fine. I've hung out in the dorms, but never a real party." JD looked up at the house that the crew was walking up to. JD could hear the music from outside, and the place already looked busy.

"Well, I guess I'm glad I'm not missing your first party," Sara said.

JD smiled, and the two of them followed the crew inside, past the crowded living room, and into the kitchen. It was cramped, and the floor was already slightly sticky.

"A lot of people came through," Dawn said to Cody.

"Yeah, Sebastian invited all his business major friends," Cody responded.

Dawn scanned the room dramatically before sighing, "Feels like a proper college rager, my friend."

Cody beamed.

The kitchen was small, but the counters were clean. Empty liquor bottles decorated the windowsill looking out onto the backyard.

"Do you guys want the surprise now or later?" Cody asked.

"Now," Dawn said, immediately. "I can't handle not knowing things."

Cody laughed and looked at Joe. "Do you want to tell them?"

"Wait, Joe, you know what it is?" Haley glared at him.

"Well," Joe started, "wait, no, you tell them!"

"Me? Okay fine," Cody said. To JD, they looked like giddy little kids.

"Jesus, guys, what is it?" Dawn demanded.

"Okay, well you know my uncle that lives in Arkansas?" Cody said, his eyebrows raised.

"Uncle Vinny?" Haley asked.

"Yeah! Well, he made us this," Cody reached into the cabinet under the sink and pulled out a large glass jar with a fabric lid and a fancy calligraphy label that read: To moonshine, crew time, and loose rhymes. - Uncle Vinny.

Dawn and Haley erupted. "No way!"

"Yeah, I told him all about freshman year when I was staying with him last summer. He got a kick out of it all. He promised us a jar of his finest moonshine, and I picked it up a couple weeks ago when I saw him."

"How is ol' Vinny?" Dawn asked.

"You know. Doing his thing. Drinking, wrestling cows, howling at the moon, probably."

"I can't believe you kept this a secret," said Haley.

"Well, almost. I told Joe because I was stressed about bringing it on a plane coming back."

"And this narc convinced you to?" Dawn said, pointing to Joe.

"Hey!" Joe retorted.

"Well, he first told me not to put it in my carry-on, so Joe thinks I'm an idiot, for the record, but then he said that he's surprised that I was stressed about it—that it was off-brand for me to be stressed about something like the TSA or underage drinking laws—and that was the motivation I needed. I was gently reminded that I'm a fearless delinquent. That I don't give a fuck. He was a real friend in that moment."

Dawn held up the jar and examined it. "I'm glad you didn't get caught! I talk a lot of shit, but I probably wouldn't smuggle moonshine on a plane. Sounds stressful."

"It wasn't too bad. I took an edible before the flight, so I wasn't stressed."

Dawn laughed. "We definitely have to toast with it," she said, excitedly.

"Just a little for me," Sara said.

"Yeah, I'm driving, so I'll try it another time," Joe said, filling a shot glass with water.

Cody poured the moonshine into tiny shot glasses. JD was hesitant to take it. He could feel the shots from earlier still hot on his cheeks. He looked around at the circle the crew had made in the kitchen, and he was suddenly very grateful to be a part of it. The feeling helped him ignore the fact that he now held another small glass of poison in his hands. Sara held the shot with her thumb and index finger like it was a worm or a piece of trash. It was about a quarter full. "Do you have chase?" she asked Cody.

"Not really…" Cody opened the fridge to look around.

Sara closed her eyes with defeat. She put the shot glass to her nose and recoiled.

"Oh! Wait!" Cody returned with a half-full jug of cranberry juice.

"Oh, thank God." Sara poured the juice into cups and passed them out.

Haley saw JD's tightened face. "JD, I have a trick for you. This is actually Sara's trick, but I think you'll need it."

Sara nodded, sagely.

Haley continued, "Before you take the shot, take a small sip of the chase." She mimed the action as she talked. "Swallow half of it, take the shot, then chase it. Makes things way easier."

JD looked at Sara and she nodded again in confirmation. They held up the shots of moonshine up together and waited expectantly. JD liked knowing the drill. Everyone looked at each other as they thought. Joe looked at JD as if prompting him to make one. JD stayed silent but furrowed his brow as if in thought.

Cody cleared his throat, "To fireworks and family perks!"

JD followed the advice told to him, but the searing, chemical taste was intolerable, and JD's face showed every bit of displeasure. He opened his eyes to see that the feeling was shared.

"God, that was awful!" Haley exclaimed.

"Hey, Uncle Vinny, worked hard on that!" Cody argued, but the grimace through which he spoke argued for him. Everyone drank the cranberry juice almost desperately, as if dousing flames with water.

"The trick normally works," Haley said through her grimace. "Unless you're drinking battery acid."

JD noticed the small amount of liquid still in Sara's glass. She shook her head and discretely poured it out into the sink. She made eye-contact with JD and shook her head, amused.

"Look who it is!" a voice broke into the kitchen. "My favorite people!"

JD looked to see a guy in a red, white and blue tank top, holding a large glass bottle of what looked like whiskey in one hand. He was tall and had almost white, blond hair shaved to a buzz cut.

"Hey Levi," Cody said. Dawn rolled her eyes as Levi joined the circle. He put his arm on her shoulder, and she shook him off.

"What are y'all drinking?" he asked.

"It's this moonshine that Cody's uncle made," Joe responded. "Let's take another one?"

Haley's response was quick, "I'm not taking another sip of that stuff." She looked at Cody, "No offense."

"I've got some of this," Levi said, holding up the handle of whiskey. "You can have some, but I'm not doing that rhyming shit you guys do."

Haley rolled her eyes, "I'm good. I'm gonna go piss actually." Without saying anything, she, Dawn, and Sara all left the kitchen.

JD wished he left with them, but he didn't move.

"Why do girls always go in groups like that?" Levi said in a scoff. "It's not like they can all go at the same time?" He started pouring the whiskey, but Joe stopped him.

"Oh, just water for me," he said.

"Really? Is this the whole running thing?" Levi asked, defensively.

Joe nodded.

"Man, you are no fun anymore."

Joe frowned.

"Dude, I'm just playing! Pour your little water shot."

Joe forced a chuckle and poured cranberry juice instead.

"This is JD," Cody introduced. JD had felt awkward standing there, but the introduction somehow made it worse.

Levi nodded, "Shot?"

JD didn't want one but nodded anyway.

Levi poured shots of the whiskey and passed them out. They clinked glasses but didn't rhyme or make a toast. JD did his best to mask his displeasure; it was the worst shot of the night.

"Let's play some pong. Grab those cups," Cody said to Joe.

"Good idea," Joe replied.

JD followed them outside where music was playing from different speakers, and people were standing around drinking from red cups. Strings of incandescent bulbs lit the patio; JD was grateful to be out of the small kitchen. They crowded around a ping pong table as Cody and Levi filled plastic cups from a large metal keg.

"You ever played?" Joe asked JD.

He shook his head.

"Pretty much just get the ball into the cups, and make sure your elbows don't go over the edge of the table. All the other dumb rules you'll pick up as we go."

They played and JD was glad to be doing something instead of just talking. He and Joe were losing, but not by a lot. Cody threw and the ball started spinning around the inner edge of the cup. Nimbly, Joe jumped and scooped it out before it hit the beer.

"Damn you, Joe," Cody said.

"So if it starts spinning," Joe said to JD, "you can grab it before it goes in, and it doesn't count. If it touches the beer, though, it does count."

"Yeah, guys finger it, and girls have to blow." Levi added, matter-of-factly. "Unless you're Cody."

Cody went red in the face.

"Dude," Cody said quietly.

"No shame, bro. I don't make the rules." Levi made his next shot into the last cup. He hollered and threw a fist into the air. Cody, still flushed, high-fived him.

The game finished and Joe and Levi teamed up for another game. Cody grabbed two new beers and handed one to JD as they sat to watch.

JD thanked him and took a sip. Quietly Cody said to him, "Sorry about the comment earlier. Levi kind of sucks. He's not a homophobe, I don't think."

"That's good! I think…" JD said.

"You and Arjun are together, right?"

"Oh, yeah we—um, I mean—we were," JD stammered.

"Sorry, I hate to pry," Cody said.

"No, it's okay. It was pretty recent." It was the truth, JD supposed.

"I'm sorry about that."

"No, it's okay. I'm sorry Levi made that comment to you."

"I'm used to it. I was just embarrassed that he made a blowjob joke about me in front of a cute guy I don't know that well." Cody chuckled, nervously.

JD, caught off-guard, choked on his beer.

"Sorry, you said it was recent," he mended.

JD didn't know what to say. On one hand, he was flustered by the attention he was getting from someone he'd idolized for a year. On the other hand, he was feeling guilty about flirting with someone within hours of breaking up with Arjun, and somehow on top of it all, stressed about asking this boy the weird embarrassing favor of vouching for him to a professor. JD opened his mouth to say something, but nothing came out.

The silence was interrupted by the whole patio chanting, "ONE TWO THREE FOUR…" JD and Cody looked to see a group of guys holding someone upside down in a handstand over the keg of beer. The spigot was inside his mouth, and he was chugging as the crowd counted.

"What the—" JD said, instinctively.

Cody laughed. "It's a keg stand. It's super uncomfortable, but the keg stand record of 45 seconds is kind of a big deal at this house. Levi obviously holds the record."

JD watched intently. Cody joined in the chanting. The guy spat it out at 25 seconds, and his friends let him down. He yelled and the crowd cheered.

"Say what you will, that's pretty impressive," Cody mused. "Although not very sanitary." He grimaced looking at the spigot of the keg.

A couple moments passed, and JD could tell that the conversation was coming to a lull. He wanted to keep talking but didn't know what to say. The small talk bubbled out, "So what brought you to Larimer University?" JD asked.

"The music program," Cody said plainly. "They offered me a pretty good gig, I couldn't refuse."

JD knew this. The department only offered one or two full rides a year—sometimes none—and it was no secret in the music building that Cody was one of them. There were even rumors that he would graduate early with scholarship prospects for grad schools on the east coast.

"Me too, it's a great program," JD responded. "I've wanted to come here pretty much my whole life. We did a field trip to the university in middle school, and when we toured the music building, even then I knew."

"You must be pretty good," Cody said.

JD cocked his head.

"I haven't actually heard you play yet, but I always see you in and out of the practice room. You must be good."

JD shook his head slightly, "Not really."

Cody raised his eyebrows.

"Arjun is way better than me."

Cody rolled his eyes.

"What?" JD asked, slightly annoyed.

"Everyone's always worried about being the best."

"You don't get to say that because you are the best. You don't know what it feels like not to be." JD said, sharply.

"That's not true," Cody said. "I actually went to a really competitive performing arts high school back home."

JD didn't interrupt.

"I used to beat myself up over everything. Nothing was ever good enough. I felt like I was falling short, and letting people down, especially my parents. They paid a lot for me to go to that school." Cody shifted in his seat. "I felt like I couldn't do anything else when I came to college, especially after the financial aid opportunities came in. I'm really glad to be where I am, but at the same time, I had to find the fun in it all to make myself sane."

"What do you mean?" JD asked.

"I found a band!" Cody laughed. "I'd be lying if I said most of my energy didn't go towards my own creative endeavors, but for some reason, putting my attention towards what I wanted to do, made me a better musician all around."

JD nodded. "You said you play the drums? Is it like a rock band?"

Cody beamed, "We're called 'Wednesday After School.' It's kind of like punk ska, meets indie folk, meets 80s cover band."

JD cocked his head.

"You'll just have to hear it then, won't you?" Cody smirked. He took another drink from his beer and looked back over at the beer pong game being played. When he did, he rested his knee against JD's and left it there. JD wanted to continue talking, but Cody's closeness was distracting. JD turned to say something but was caught off-guard by the smell of Cody's cologne; JD took a sip of beer, and the malty liquid doused the scent from his nose. JD couldn't help but chuckle at how nervous and silly he felt.

"What?" Cody asked.

"Nothing; I like your cologne!"

He smiled, and JD went red. Cody turned his body and leaned closer to JD. He opened his mouth to say something, but JD panicked and blurted, "Can I ask you a favor?"

Cody nodded. JD wished he'd stayed quiet but decided that there was no turning back.

"I was wondering if… well you see I got kicked out of the program tonight. It's a long story, but it's because I didn't show up to the concert."

As JD rambled, Cody's eyes hardened to concern. He turned even more towards JD, but pulled his knee in.

"I wouldn't normally tell you all of this—not that you wouldn't find out—I mean, maybe. It's just I have to make an appeal to get back in, and I was wondering," JD wanted to stop himself, but his mouth wouldn't stop, "well because Dr. Cleary is the director, and I know you don't really know me, but if you could talk to her and vouch for me, maybe." JD was beet-red, and humiliated. The look of confusion and pity on Cody's face had answered for him.

"Look, JD, I'm just an undergrad. I don't really have any kind of say. I mean, I'm really sorry about all of this. It really sucks, I just—"

"No, it's fine," JD interrupted. "Really."

Cody didn't say anything for a moment. "Is that why you came tonight?"

JD was caught off-guard by the question. It wasn't, but he'd be lying if he said it hadn't been on his mind during the party. He wanted to take back everything he'd said. The confession and plea stayed stagnant in the air. JD wanted to refute everything, but he knew that the truth was that he did want something from Cody. JD knew that the truth was that he was selfish, just like Arjun said.

JD had managed to shake his head, but Cody frowned. "Well, I can't really help you." Cody said, more hurt than cold.

JD fumbled a weak apology, "Sorry, I—"

Cody stood up, "I think I'm going to go jump in on another game. Enjoy the party." He walked over to the ping pong table and didn't look back.

JD was hot with embarrassment. He hadn't thought about how the request would come off, and he felt stupid. He stood up to leave. JD wanted to disappear. He didn't want to face Joe or the others and tell them what happened. He walked inside and inched his way through the crowd towards the front door. He made it to the entryway when he heard a familiar voice.

"Where are you going?" Haley asked.

"I think I'm going to head out," JD said, trying to sound casual.

"Wait what?"

"Yeah, I'm just kind of beat. Say bye to everyone for me."

"This is because you read the letter?" Haley said, curtly.

JD turned around.

"I saw you rip it up at the park. I told you; you shouldn't have read it. You promised—"

"Haley, it's not about that. I'm just tired." Frustration bubbled under the words. JD couldn't help but notice people around them starting to stare, privy to the tension.

"C'mon, you should stay," Haley demanded. "Who cares about that other guy? People get dumped all the time, JD, it doesn't matter what that letter says—"

"Just shut up!" JD snapped. His blood was searing, and his face was hot.

Haley scowled, "Well excuse me for trying to help. Jesus."

"I didn't ask for your help! Just mind your business."

Haley crossed her arms.

"What's going on?" Sara walked up to the two of them and put her hand on Haley's shoulder.

"Apparently, I'm a bitch for wanting to help," Haley murmured.

Sara looked at JD and back to Haley.

"I'm gonna go," JD said.

"Haley," Sara said "I think Dawn's looking for you in the kitchen. I'm going to make sure JD has a ride."

Haley rolled her eyes and stomped away.

JD started to open the door.

"Wait," Sara said to JD, "you should come with me."

"I just want to leave. I should've left earlier."

"Trust me." Sara gestured to the stairs. After Haley left, most of the eyes had followed her, but JD still felt the tension around him. "I want to show you something before you leave. Trust me."

JD waited a moment. The anger in him still burned, but he felt, for some reason, that he'd owed Sara this—whatever it was. JD let go of the doorknob and followed Sara through the crowd and upstairs.

"Such Great Heights"
by The Postal Service

The music from the party echoed throughout the house, but the upstairs felt much quieter. The hallway was empty, and all of the doors were closed, but Sara opened one and led JD through a well-kept bedroom to a large window already half open. Sara opened it all the way and started climbing out. It led onto a section of the roof overlooking the backyard. JD followed her; he was confused but didn't say anything. The cool evening air felt good against his hot and humiliated skin. They sat next to each other on the sloped, gritty tiles. They could hear the music and chatter from the patio, but the roof extended far enough that no one could see them up there. JD wondered if Cody was on the patio again. He listened for his voice but couldn't distinguish it.

A long moment passed before JD said, "Thanks for getting me out of there. I should still probably go though."

Sara nodded but said, "I wanted to grab you before you did." She waited another couple seconds before adding, "I couldn't let your first party experience end like that. Doesn't sit right with me."

"I appreciate that."

"What happened with Haley, anyway? Did you really call her a bitch?" Sara asked.

JD's reaction was quick and defensive, "No, I didn't—"

"I figured." Sara said. "She can be a little dramatic when she's drunk."

"I mean, I didn't call her any names, but I was definitely a dick to her."

"What happened?" Sara repeated.

"It's dumb. Apparently, she saw me open the envelope earlier, and I wanted to leave, but she wanted me to stay."

Sara paused before asking, "Do you want to talk about it?"

JD didn't want to tell her any of the embarrassing details. "I just feel everything has gone wrong tonight, and I just keep hurting people, somehow. I'm just selfish.

"I don't think that's true," Sara said. "Besides, I don't think Haley is really that upset. I mean, she is tonight, but not at you. Not really."

JD looked at her.

"She likes you a lot. She was really excited that you were coming out, and that's another reason I grabbed you. She's kind of drunk and already on edge, so I feel like if you guys talked, it would smooth over really easily. I'd hate for you to leave, and for that small fight to linger longer than it has to."

JD thought for a moment. "Why is she on edge?"

"It's hard for her to party with Levi. They used to date, and he sucks. We all hate him."

"I could tell earlier."

"Yeah. Haley also found out recently that Levi has an old polaroid of her from when they were dating. He keeps it in his wallet."

"That actually sounds kind of sweet?" JD inquired.

"Except that in the photo she's topless, and apparently Levi shows it off at frat parties and stuff."

"Oh, that's terrible!"

"We hate him."

"I can see why."

"So she's been stressed about that all night. Levi is really good friends with Cody, so she doesn't want to make it a big deal."

"But it is a big deal!" JD protested. "He sucks."

"I agree, but Haley's really embarrassed about it, and doesn't want Joe to find out."

"Why?"

"I don't know… Joe is pretty cool with Levi. Or at least wants to be. We all used to hang out, and Joe really wants things to be like they were then."

JD nodded.

"It's not like the rest of us don't miss it—or part of it at least. I think he feels left out sometimes. He lives with some old running friends, which I think is good for him, but it's not the same as living in the dorms with everyone. It can be hard wanting to be in two places at once." Sara chuckled to herself. "Anyway. Haley doesn't want Joe to know about the photo. She wants to ignore it all, and Joe would want to fix things. He's a really good guy."

JD nodded. "It sucks that she has to deal with all of that tonight. And some new guy yelling at her and telling her to mind her own business." Sullen with guilt, he looked at Sara.

She chuckled. "I'm sure if you talk to her, she'll be fine. I'm sorry that she was pressuring you to stay. She can be a lot sometimes."

JD nodded, thinking about it. "It's okay. I mean, it's nice of her to want me to stay. I've just had kind of a crazy night."

"Her heart's always in the right place. She just won't take no for an answer if she thinks she's right about something."

"Joe warned me about her superpower."

"Call it what you will, but it's a blessing and a curse. It's infuriating at times, but then again, it's why I'm here tonight." Sara looked at JD. "If it wasn't for Haley, I'd be home asleep."

"Me too!" JD added.

Sara smiled. "Like I said, it's a blessing and a curse, but for what it's worth, I'm grateful to have a friend that gets me out. She lives her life in a way worth talking about later—like she does things and sees things in a way that warrants telling a story about it. If I think about it too hard, I get a pang of jealousy, but it always melts away into some kind of admiration. And appreciation, I suppose. I am, after all, a part of a lot of those stories."

JD didn't say anything for a bit. He tried to picture himself doing the things that Haley had done that night. He pictured himself snatching a letter out of a stranger's hand or yelling on a stump. He tried to imagine his own face on a fake ID. It felt impossible. He then imagined it was Haley sitting on the roof next to Sara instead. He tried to picture what she would say when she went downstairs, but he couldn't. "Do you mind if we hang out here for a little longer? I don't know if I'm ready to face anyone yet."

"Of course! Cody lets me sneak away up here at parties. Big groups really aren't my thing, and sneaking away to hang out in some room feels kind of sad, you know? Also—" Sara reached into her pocket and pulled out her phone, "I get to pick the music up here. I've made a whole playlist of rooftop songs." She showed him her phone with the playlist. It was titled: Rooftop Songs and had a picture of what looked like the exact view they were looking at. "It's a running title," she said.

"What's a rooftop song?" JD asked.

Sara shrugged. "Could be a lot of things. Could be on the nose—songs about rooftops or summits of some kind. A lot of times it's music to listen to when you're avoiding people at a party and chilling here." She played a song and placed it down between them. "But mostly, its songs for looking at all of this…" she gestured upwards towards the sky.

JD laughed and the two of them leaned back facing the starlit sky above them. The moon was just a sliver still hanging low on the horizon. They stayed there for a while, not talking, but listening to the song that played and the indiscernible chatter from the patio. At one point, a nearby house lit a firecracker, and the explosion was followed by a roar of cheers from the party below. JD thought again about Arjun and what he might be doing, but before he could dwell any longer, he heard the window behind him slide open.

"Hey!" JD heard Cody's voice say. "I thought you'd be up here, Sara."

"Hey Cody," she said, sitting up. JD followed her lead and looked worriedly at Cody.

"I see Sara showed you the best seat in the house." Cody said to JD, with a disarmingly warm smile. He climbed out of the window and sat next to them.

JD nodded. The waves of guilt returned, but Cody didn't seem to notice.

"I love this song," Cody said. "Is this your rooftop playlist?"

Sara smiled, "Yeah. I couldn't tell if it was too on the nose or not, but I feel like it fits the vibe."

"Oh definitely." Cody leaned back onto his palms and took a long, deep breath. "I should come out here with you more often."

"How is it in there?" Sara asked.

"Oh good. I am very proud of the turn out, but it was hard to find somewhere to take a breather."

"I've never known you to need a breather from a party." Sara said, squinting at Cody.

He grinned sheepishly, "Okay you got me. By 'breather' I mean this." He pulled out a joint from the pocket in his shirt. "I knew if I lit this bad boy on the patio, it'd be cashed before it made its way back around to me."

Sara laughed.

"It's true! It's my last one, and it's against stoner law not to pass to whomever asks. You know? I can't be stingy, so I'm gonna be secretive and only smoke with my two friends on the roof. That feels chill right?"

Sara laughed again. "Your secret is safe with me! Although I probably won't smoke tonight."

"I respect that." Cody said, lighting the joint. "JD, what about you?"

JD shook his head. "No thanks." JD was caught off guard by Cody's nonchalance and warmth. It was hard for JD to picture Cody saying anything rude or snide, but it was almost as if the embarrassing and hurtful conversation from earlier hadn't happened.

"Oh no, more for me," Cody joked.

"I wish I could smoke at parties," Sara said. "Whenever I try though, I get really anxious and paranoid. It definitely ruins my night."

"I remember you telling me about that," Cody said, taking a hit. "What does Dawn call it?"

"The 'oofs!' I get the 'oofs,'"

"Oh yeah! I remember we were all at your house one night smoking, and Dawn just looks up at everyone and asks, 'Do you ever get like… oof!' and then describes being paranoid about everything."

Sara nodded, "I get the 'oofs' a lot, especially in big groups. If I get too high, I just feel like everything is going wrong. It sucks, but I love the term. I can just tell you guys I have the 'oofs' and go to bed or hang out alone. It's a good out."

The musky scent wafted in the air. JD didn't like the smell, but he liked the way the smoke left Cody's lips. The soft orange glow of the lit joint burned brighter as he inhaled. JD thought of it like a tiny sunset burning and fading with each breath. He didn't want to be caught staring and averted his gaze towards the sky.

Cody commented, "So what's all this stars versus fireworks nonsense I hear Haley and Joe prattling on about all night?"

Sara chuckled, "It's a steadfast romantic standing his ground against a blunt yet fickle force of nature."

"I can't possibly imagine what you mean," Cody said.

"I just mean that Joe is too sappy to say anything against the stars, and Haley only believes what she's saying because it's getting a rise out of Joe."

JD nodded in agreement.

"Harsh!" Cody laughed, taking another hit.

"Honest," Sara retorted. "They do this all the time. Always have."

"That's true," Cody said. "I'd like to put myself in the sappy, romantic side of that Venn diagram, but Haley is too hard to disagree with."

Sara nodded.

"Is she okay tonight?" Cody asked, taking another hit.

"She's been better," Dawn said.

"That would be mostly my fault," JD confessed.

Cody raised his eyebrows.

"She's one of the many that I owe an apology to tonight." JD looked at Cody as he said it.

"I don't think you owe as many as you think," Cody responded.

JD smiled. A moment passed and Cody said, "Where do you guys stand on the stars debate?"

"Oh, we're definitely on Joe's side. I honestly don't think anyone is really on Haley's." Sara added. "Are you coming up to Horsetooth tonight? I think Joe is dead set on stargazing tonight."

"No, I should probably stay. Don't want to abandon the party in case something stupid happens."

"I heard a rumor that you might punch a hole in a wall tonight?" JD quipped.

"Who said that? Dawn?"

JD shrugged.

"You throw one beer bottle at a brick wall once and suddenly you're some crazy, wild child." Cody was grinning at himself.

"I don't know, Cody, you are kind of crazy." Sara looked to JD. "You should hear his theory on the moon."

"Okay, now we're coming for my beliefs?"

Sara laughed. "If you could call a crazy conspiracy theory a 'belief!'"

"Wait what?" JD said.

Cody looked at him, and JD noticed the amusement in his eyes. "My highly researched theory on the moon…"

"Highly." Sara said, mimicking the joint being smoked. JD laughed.

Cody dramatically cleared his throat. "My *theory* is that the moon is *not* a natural satellite like other moons in the solar system. Rocks or asteroids that eventually start orbiting planets. No. Our moon is too perfect. Close enough to move the tides, but far enough not to mess with gravity and stuff? Perfect distance and size to make perfect solar eclipses? The perfect rotation to only see one side? Also, one time an asteroid hit it, and apparently it rang like a bell. Like it was hollow. I don't know, it seems fishy to me…"

"Wait, if it's not a natural satellite, then who put it there?" JD asked in earnest.

Cody grinned, "Many people would say aliens—"

"'Many people,'" Sara mocked with air quotes.

Cody cleared his throat again, "But I think it's humans from the future."

"Why would they—"

"I don't have all the answers JD, only some of them."

"I don't think you actually believe it," Sara asserted. "I think you're like Haley with the debate. You're just trying to get a rise out of people; I can see it in your eyes."

"What you're seeing in my eyes, Sara, is this joint." He held up the joint. "What you're hearing from my mouth, is the truth." As he said it, he pulled the rest of the joint to his lips, pulled hard, and sucked the whole thing into his mouth. After a moment, he swallowed, and the joint was gone.

"Did you just eat that?" JD asked, bewildered.

"Yeah, it's called 'eating the roach,'" he said calmly.

"See?" Sara exclaimed, "Crazy!"

Cody grinned wider. JD thought about Dawn's story about her friend Lee, and what Sara had said earlier about Haley. He thought that Cody must be like Haley in the way that he lives his life in order to tell the story. Or maybe Cody just lived in the way that made others want to tell stories about him.

"Oh! I almost forgot!" Cody said. "I didn't know what your vibe was, but I thought I'd bring some reinforcements." Cody reached back through the window without moving from where he sat. He pulled from inside the handle of whiskey and two shot glasses. "Sorry, I only brought two, but it would be my pleasure to drink from the handle."

"Thanks, Cody," Sara said, "but I might be tapped out for the night."

JD nodded, "Me too."

Cody smirked. "Well, I thought you might say that." He reached back into the window, his t-shirt riding up his side as he strained. "So I brought this too, just in case." He held up a small, square plastic bottle full of blue liquid.

"Is that Pedialyte?" Sara asked. "Cody, that is so thoughtful."

He beamed. "Two shots of Pedialyte, coming right up." Cody poured the glasses and passed them out. JD and Sara held the glasses up to the bottle of whiskey that Cody held. Soundlessly, they waited for an idea for a cheers.

It surprised even himself, when JD spoke up. "I've got one…" He cleared his throat in preparation. "To neon lights and natural satellites!" They drank, and the salty-sweet liquid was delicious compared to the alcohol from earlier in the night.

"That was a good one," Cody said.

"Thanks!"

Cody's phone buzzed and the white light lit up his face. "Oh no. I think some freshman is puking in the bathtub."

"Oh no, I'm sorry Cody." Sara consoled.

He smiled, "Eh, I puked in my fair share of inconvenient places my freshman year. I'm honestly happy to oblige."

He stood to walk back through the window when Sara stopped him. "Cody, when I say crazy, I want you to know I mean it, but in truly the best way possible."

He beamed at her. "I know."

"Sober"

by Childish Gambino

When Cody left, Sara turned to JD, "He likes you."

JD looked at Sara, mouth agape.

"He's a good guy," Sara added. "And so pretty."

JD rolled his eyes. "I don't know if this will come as a surprise to you, but he's kind of like a small-town celebrity in the music building. He's really good."

"That doesn't surprise me at all. You should ask him out."

"How do you know I like him?" JD retorted.

"It's a little obvious," Sara said, bluntly.

"I guess it's just a little complicated. I actually got broken up with tonight."

Sara's face didn't change.

"You knew?"

"Haley told me." Sara replied. "She can't keep a secret. It was also part of her pitch to get me to come out with you guys."

"Wait what?" JD asked, more amused than upset.

"Yeah. She made it sound like some big crusade to turn your night around, and that I had a huge role in that."

JD laughed.

"She's ridiculous, but she is convincing."

"So you see how that makes the Cody thing complicated?"

Sara nodded. "Yes and no."

"What would you do?"

"Do you want what I'd actually do, or what I like to think I'd do?"

"Both."

"I like to think I'd seize the opportunity and get a new boyfriend the same day I lost one."

JD laughed again. "And what would you actually do?"

"Nothing, but post about it on my Tumblr." Sara smiled at herself.

"You're still on Tumblr?"

"Everyday." Sara said plainly. "Although it's more like a daily journaling thing now as opposed to a social media thing."

JD nodded.

"I am glad I came out tonight, though. This feels like a night I want to actually be there for."

"What do you mean?"

She continued, "I bail a lot. And not necessarily in a bad way. I love to be alone. But sometimes when Haley or Dawn tell stories, they include me in it, even if I wasn't there. I don't know if they do it on purpose, or if they just forget; most of the time it's nice to be retroactively included, but it is a reminder to myself that I wasn't there. And sometimes I wish that I was."

JD nodded.

"And tonight feels like one I want to be here for."

"Well, I'm glad you are. And I'm glad I am too, honestly," JD said.

Sara smiled at him. "Are you going to talk to Haley?"

JD thought again about what Haley might say in his position. He couldn't picture at all what she would say, but it dawned on him the crazy thing that Haley might do. "Yeah, and I think I have an idea for how to make it up to her," he replied.

Sara cocked her head.

"It's kind of out there, but it just might work."

"Okay," Sara said hesitantly.

JD smiled. "I think we'll need Dawn's help too."

The two made their way back through the window and to the balcony at the top of the stairs. They saw Haley and Dawn talking near the kitchen.

"Okay," started JD, "I need you to distract Haley for a bit. I'm going to be on the patio with Dawn, and I don't want her to see."

Sara looked worriedly at JD. "Are you sure about this?"

JD wasn't but nodded.

Sara went down first, said something to Haley, and walked with her through the crowd into a room JD didn't know. When Dawn started to follow, Sara turned to her and pointed up at JD at the balcony. Dawn looked confused but walked upstairs anyway.

"What's going on?" Dawn asked, bluntly.

"I'm gonna need you to trust me. I've got kind of a crazy idea, but I need your help."

Dawn looked skeptically at JD. Through squinted eyes, Dawn said, "Alright. Lead the way."

JD led her down the stairs and out the back doors onto the patio. It was still crowded. JD looked around and when he saw Levi, he turned to Dawn, "Okay. We need to go talk to Levi."

"Oh no way—" Dawn protested.

"Trust me," JD insisted. "I've got a plan."

They walked over and JD stood near them. Levi was talking to two other guys that JD didn't know, and all of JD's confidence flitted away as he stood there, unsure of how to insert himself. Amused, Dawn walked closer and entered the conversation seamlessly. She put her arm on one of the guy's shoulders and made a quick-witted jab at what Levi was wearing. Levi laughed and replied, "Good to see you still hate me."

Dawn shrugged and JD entered the conversation next to her.

"I heard about your keg stand record," JD said.

"Levi smirked, "Undefeated."

"What was it? Twenty-five seconds?"

Levi's friend came to his defense. "Who'd you hear that from? His record is forty-five."

"Forty-five?" JD's feigned bewilderment was only discernible to Dawn; he could see her smirk in his periphery. "I don't think that's possible."

"Well, you better believe it," Levi said.

"I'm with JD, I'll believe it when I see it," Dawn added.

"You did see it!" Levi said, frustration in his tone. "You were there!"

Dawn made a doubtful face.

"Forty-five seconds is too long of a time," JD said. "I bet you can't do it again."

Levi's eyes narrowed at JD, "I'll do it again, but you have to do it first."

All the blood left JD's face. He knew his plan was half-baked, but he hadn't considered this possibility. He swallowed and nodded.

"And to make things more interesting, the loser has to wear his shirt like he just made the bitch cup."

The confusion on JD's face was evident.

"The bitch cup? In Beer Pong? If you make the middle cup first, you have to wear your shirt like a bra." Levi explained. His friend demonstrated by pulling up the bottom of his shirt and tucking it into the front of his neckline. "You have to wear it like that all night."

"You mean the loser has to," JD corrected.

"I said what I said."

They followed Levi to the keg, and Dawn nudged JD with a look on her face that prodded for more information. *Trust me,* mouthed JD.

"You first," Levi said. JD cringed slightly at the sight of the spigot.

"Okay, hold on," JD said, tucking his shirt into his jeans.

"Everyone's gonna see anyway, princess, you might as well show 'em now!" Levi slapped JD's stomach as he said it. Dawn rolled her eyes. JD grabbed the keg with both hands and took a deep breath. In one motion, Levi hoisted up his legs. When JD was upside down, Dawn put the spigot in his mouth and asked if he was ready. JD could see a crowd already forming, and felt hot, not just from the blood rushing to his head, but from all the eyes already on him. Hesitantly, he nodded.

Dawn turned the valve and JD could hear the chorus of counting start as the bubbly liquid filled his mouth. It was cold and jarring at first, but after almost choking on the first few swallows, JD found the rhythm and kept chugging. Despite the embarrassing and vulnerable position, the loud chanting was motivating. JD found the chugging tolerable for about fifteen seconds but powered through five more before shaking his head. Dawn grabbed the spigot and JD was let down.

JD was met with cheers from the spectators but felt only the bubbly pressure of twenty seconds worth of beer in his stomach. "Alright, you're up," JD said confidently to Levi.

Levi almost scoffed as he grabbed the keg. "Alright lift me up if you can."

JD ignored the dig and hoisted him up. Dawn, with disgust apparent on her face, put the spigot in Levi's mouth. As the crowd chanted, JD gestured for Dawn to help hold Levi up. Reluctantly, as if grabbing a wet dog, Dawn held the other side. JD slowly began to shift his body, chanting with the crowd as he did. Dawn's brow was furrowed with confusion, until she noticed JD discretely reaching for the wallet in Levi's back pocket.

Caught up on the plan, Dawn joined the chanting and began heckling Levi. The count had reached thirty seconds when the wallet slowly fell out of the pocket, and into the crook of JD's arm. Everyone was watching Levi's face as he continued to chug. Once the count reached fifty, Levi spat out the spigot and began to writhe. Dawn and JD quickly let him down, and by the time Levi pushed himself off the keg upright, JD had slipped the wallet into his own pocket.

Levi hollered and threw his fist in the air. "Woo! New record, baby!" He turned to JD. "A deal's a deal, bro."

JD forced his grimace into a smile and nodded. He looked around and saw every eye on him. He pictured himself giving the wallet to Haley in hopes to motivate or distract his mind, but what helped was picturing Haley on the stump from earlier. The way she yelled and didn't care who heard or what they thought. In a swift motion, JD pulled his shirt up and tucked it into his neckline. The punishment was silly, and JD forced himself to feel silly instead of humiliated. He forced another grin and shook Levi's hand.

Dawn grabbed JD's arm and started leading him back into the house. He looked at her and could see her lips pulled into her mouth suppressing laughter. When they turned a corner into the kitchen Dawn let out a howl. "You genius! You mad man!" Dawn was beaming as she punched JD in the arm.

JD couldn't help but grin as wide as his face would let him.

"I've always wanted to be a part of a heist. What a crazy plan. Was I the honeypot? God, how fun. Who's next?"

JD laughed. "I still can't believe it worked. It only cost my dignity and probably an hour's worth of puking later."

"Well, I'm impressed. God, that felt good. I'm so amped!"

"I should probably go find Haley."

Dawn looked at JD and smiled. "She'll be really happy to see you."

JD didn't believe her, but the way she had said it reassured JD more than he had expected. He nodded.

"I think she's in the garage with Sara. I'm gonna go find Joe. I feel like we should get out of here soon."

JD nodded and walked to the garage. When he opened the door, only Haley and Sara were there. They sat on a dingy couch, each holding what looked like glasses of water.

"Hey," JD interrupted. "Mind if I steal Haley?"

"Not at all," Sara said. "I'll go find Dawn."

JD nodded and sat down next to Haley. "Listen, I'm sorry about earlier. You were just trying to—"

"No, JD, it's okay—"

"Seriously. It wasn't cool of me to snap like that. I have kind of a temper, and you were just trying to be a good friend. I wanted to make it up to you."

"You don't have to."

"Well, I already did."

"Please tell me it's the outfit, because I'm tickled by the image of you walking through the house like that."

JD laughed. "Well, I'm glad my humiliation amuses you!" JD reached into his pocket. "Don't be mad that Sara told me. I just thought it would be a good way to make up for yelling at you. You were trying to be a good friend to me, even though we just met, so I wanted to be a good friend to you."

He pulled out the wallet and handed it to her. Curiously, Haley opened it and gasped when she realized what it was. "Did you steal this?"

JD shrugged, noncommittally.

Haley let out a squeal of amusement. "I cannot believe you stole this!"

"It was quite the heist. Dawn helped."

Haley searched through and found the polaroid. She held it up and smiled. "I really liked this picture." She held it for JD to see.

JD blushed and nodded.

"It's not that I give a shit who sees my tits. I'm just going to be the one that shows them, you know?"

"Yeah, he sucks."

She put the picture in her pocket and held up the wallet. "I guess we should probably just leave this laying around for him to find, huh?"

JD raised his eyebrows.

Haley gasped. "You're not suggesting…"

JD shrugged again.

Haley looked inside. "You know what. If I steal this $20 and then leave the wallet laying around, he'll find it and know that it was me because the picture is gone."

"Oh yeah."

"But he'd have to admit that he knows it's me because he's a scumbag that kept my nude in his wallet. And if I'm being honest, I would fucking love for him to know that I stole from him."

JD grinned. "The perfect crime?"

Haley smiled. "You didn't have to do this, JD. I know that today was rough, and I can be kind of obtuse to how people feel. Rather, I guess I know how people feel, I just ignore it sometimes."

"No, it's okay. I'm glad that you dragged me out tonight. To be honest, I think I've known for a long time that Arjun and I weren't going to work out."

Haley turned to JD and pushed her hair behind her ears. "What do you mean?"

"Things just haven't been the same since we came to college. We used to play and practice together. We even used to write songs for each other." JD reached into his pocket and pulled out the ripped pieces of the song. "This was what was in the envelope." He handed the pieces to Haley. "It's the first song I wrote for him. I guess he doesn't want it anymore." Tears started to well in JD's eyes.

Haley held the pieces in her hand and examined them. She started to put them back together as she spoke, "You know, for a while I was really glad that Levi still had my photo… Not that it's the same—it's not—but after a while, and when it was clear that the photo didn't mean to him what it used to, I wanted it back."

"And the fact that he showed people."

"That sucked, but what I think hurt the most was feeling like the photo was just some nude to him. That it was some hot girl, and not the girl he was, at least at one point, in love with."

JD nodded.

"I guess what I'm saying is that it sucks that Arjun gave this back, but in time you might be grateful to have it. You know? I feel like we want to leave the best of what we gave so it's what we're remembered by, but it hurts to see the most intimate pieces of ourselves become less meaningful to someone—even if it is just because of time." Haley looked up from the pieces in her lap. "With Levi, it's not so much the photo. He was the first person I had sex with, and it was really special. I thought I'd always feel that way, even if we broke up, but with the way that he treated my photo when we did, it just made me feel like it's no longer something special to him—or never was." Haley restacked the pieces neatly and handed them back. She smiled weakly at JD.

JD mustered one back but still felt like crying. "I feel like I left too many ugly things for him to hold on to," JD paused. "I'm sad that he won't have this to see and remember that I loved him. I want him to see this and think of me, that same way that everything seems to remind me of him. I've just been a terrible boyfriend lately. I've been so jealous and bitter, and I hurt him so badly tonight. What if he gets rid of the other good things? I don't want him to forget. I just left him with too many ugly, horrible things, and what if those are all that's left?"

JD wrestled with the tears, not letting them fall. Haley put her hand on his knee. When he sniffed and wiped his nose with his wrist, Haley said, "You can cry, it's okay. Really, I will be thrilled not to be the only pretty girl in a crop top that cried at this party. JD looked down at his shirt still folded in on itself. It made him laugh and he unwrapped it. The joke helped settle the stinging in his eyes.

"I don't know what to say," Haley started. "Just that I think you should hold onto that song. Don't throw it away. Promise."

He looked down at the pieces. "It really does look like garbage, doesn't it?"

"Except that it's not." Haley's eyes were sad and serious.

JD nodded. "Okay, I'll keep it." He replaced the pieces into his pocket, and once again tried to forget that the song was there. JD hadn't followed Haley's advice from earlier when he opened the envelope; he decided this time that he would.

"Spaceherosuits"
by Those Dancing Days

As JD and Haley walked towards the kitchen, Cody caught JD, "Hey, JD, can I talk to you?"

"I'll be in the kitchen," Haley said.

JD nodded.

"I heard you went for the record," Cody said.

"Yeah, I only hit twenty. Levi beat his own record though."

"Hey, I don't think keg stands should be a competition. It's all about the personal journey, you know?"

"The journey?"

"Yeah! Just you and the keg. Pushing the limits of the human body. It really is a beautiful thing."

"You're crazy."

Cody smiled. After a moment he said, "And look, I'm sorry I can't help you with Dr. Cleary. I didn't mean to react the way I did earlier. You must be really stressed; I get it."

JD shook his head, "No, don't apologize. I'm cringing just thinking about how I asked you to do that. Forget that I asked." JD was looking down at the ground.

"And I know you have a lot on your mind," Cody said, "but I want you to have this." Cody reached into his pocket and handed him a slip of paper.

"Is that your number on a piece of paper?" JD asked. "You know we have phones. We can just put in the contacts or text each other?"

"Are you making fun of me?" Cody grinned, holding back the slip of paper.

"No, it's sweet—" JD reached for it.

"Well, if that's what I get for being charming?"

"It is charming! I'll text you," JD assured.

"You better!" Cody handed him the number. "I think the crew is getting ready to head up to Horsetooth, but you're welcome to stay here if you want."

"Thanks, but I think I'll go with them." JD fumbled for an excuse. "There's the whole stars debate that they need me for."

Cody laughed. "Can't miss that!" Cody's face was close to JD's. "Well, good night, JD."

"Good night," JD said. He thought for a moment that Cody might kiss him, but he just winked and let his hand brush against JD's as he walked past.

He turned around and walked backwards, "Say hello to the stars for me!" He gestured upwards, dramatically.

JD smiled and nodded. He then found his way to the kitchen where the rest of the crew was waiting.

"Hey!" Haley said to JD. "So, we're going to settle this silly 'debate' once and for all. Joe knows I'm right."

Joe rolled his eyes. "I just think we should go stargazing tonight. With the neon sign and the fireworks, all you've had to say is how much better they are than the stars themselves. I think we need to give them a chance tonight too. It's only fair."

"Exactly," Haley said. "One last ditch effort to prove me wrong, only to be woefully disappointed when you don't."

"Well, I think the crew needs to see both sides of the argument before deciding to make you buy us all pizza." Joe crossed his arms.

"I don't know how we got wrapped up in all of this," Dawn said.

"We need an unbiased jury," Joe said.

Dawn raised her eyebrows, "I am so biased."

"Okay, I don't mean unbiased. Just the only opinions we really care about."

Dawn smiled at that. "Okay, but I'm pretty hungry so we should make this quick."

The five of them piled into the car again. Haley sat up front and passed the aux cord to Dawn as Joe pulled out onto the road. Haley put the heater on and rolled all the windows down.

"I'm excited to head up to the ridge. I feel like we haven't been in like a year," Joe said.

"Actually, I think Haley, Sara, and I went up recently," Dawn said.

Haley nodded.

"Wait, why didn't you guys text me?" Joe asked.

"Oh yeah, it was the middle of the night," Haley explained. "Besides, we're heading up now."

"I think that was just you guys," Sara said. "I'm pretty sure I went to bed."

"Hmm," Haley said.

Joe didn't say anything.

JD rested his head on the open window. He watched as the car casted shadows from the white light of the streetlamps. The shadows would start from behind the car and zoom forward into the dim black ahead of them. He watched this process repeat a couple of times, before his stomach reminded him of all the beer he drank. JD looked back inside and saw everyone looking at him.

"What?"

"Nothing, you just looked so focused," Dawn laughed.

"I think I'm drunker than I thought," JD confessed.

"A twenty second keg stand would do that," Dawn said.

"Twenty seconds?" Sara's eyes widened.

JD nodded.

"JD, I can't believe you did a keg stand," Haley said.

"Honestly me neither," he replied.

"We shotgunned beers at Cody's house last time, and even just one beer was going to make me hurl," Haley said. "Joe is kind of a shotgun champion. He can do it in like three seconds."

Joe smiled in the rearview mirror and JD could see the deep creases it made on his cheeks and around his eyes. He was the kind of person whose whole face smiled when he did.

"Well not anymore," Joe added. "Unless it's like a canned kombucha, I guess I could do that."

Haley grimaced. "Oh God, I think that's even worse!"

"Coward," Joe teased.

As they drove out of the city, JD reached into his pocket to grab the slip of paper that had Cody's number. He didn't know if he'd text him yet, but he wanted to see it again. The warm anticipation was extinguished by the sight of a fragment of his song in his hand instead of the number. JD emptied his pocket and found the slip amongst the ripped pieces. His face tightened. At first, JD thought he was angry again at Arjun for breaking up with him and giving him back the song, but as he stared at the mess in his lap, he realized that he felt guilty. He felt guilty for trying to light the kindling of something already on fire—he was still in love with Arjun; he was still angry about everything—and it seared. He knew that Arjun was still dealing with the burns JD had left him with, and JD felt terrible for wanting to text Cody before even texting his apology to Arjun. JD had felt like he had nothing to say to Arjun when he opened the envelope, but he knew that he owed him an apology.

He replaced all of the paper into his pocket and pulled out his phone instead. He drafted a text to Arjun. It was an apology mostly for what he'd done at the concert, but it was also an apology for the way everything had ended. JD remembered all of the bitter and jealous thoughts he'd had the past year and knew that in some way Arjun had to have felt it—he had to have known. Arjun didn't deserve any of that. JD looked back on the message and clicked send.

In a matter of minutes, they were entirely out of the city and driving along a winding mountain road. Without the streetlights, Joe turned on the brights and illuminated the dark asphalt ahead of them. The car followed the road, and Joe took the turns slowly and carefully. As they neared the top of the ridge, the road curved to reveal a wide and unobstructed view of the city's lights. He slowed even more, and JD admired the soft glow that the collective lights casted on the sky above it. It was a mix of yellow and white light in a faint clustered line across the horizon. JD imagined the whole horizon as a vast black marble floor and the lights being swept up by a giant broom leaving only the glowing stubborn specks at the base of the dustbin. The thought made him smile to himself.

JD wanted to say something about the view but thought about the debate. He knew that it would be a card in favor of Haley. He thought that it was a silly reason not to say something but didn't anyway. Joe seemed to read his mind when he said, "Okay, we can stop and look at the city, but we're going to go a little bit deeper into the mountains to get the best view of the sky."

"Whatever you say, Captain." Haley gave a dramatic salute. Joe pulled the car over onto the shoulder and everyone piled out. They sat on the highway cliff rail and marveled at the sight. The stars were barely visible above the skyline.

No one said anything for a minute, but Joe broke the silence, "I feel like this looks different than it did years ago. I feel like there are more white lights than yellow."

"There are," Dawn said. "Those are the LED lights. They're more energy efficient than incandescent lights."

"That's good." Joe was still staring out. "Do you miss the yellow though?"

Dawn looked out but shook her head. "I don't think so, no."

"I don't know. I feel like everything looks different from when we were kids. I remember looking out my window as a kid, especially when it rained or snowed, everything was cast in that yellow hue." Joe shifted his weight on the railing. "Now, more and more streets are that cold, fluorescent white… Does that make you sad?"

"You really do hate change, don't you?" Haley interrupted.

Joe frowned. "I— I don't think so. Excuse me for being sentimental."

"I'm not mad at you," Haley said. "I just think something can be different from what it was before and still be beautiful."

Joe didn't break his gaze from the horizon. "It can be beautiful, and I can still be sad about it."

Haley didn't say anything for a moment. She nodded and then said, "You're right. Sorry. That was a shitty thing to say."

Joe nodded.

"Maybe it makes it more special," Haley said. "The fact that you grew up with the lights different than they are now. Like how they put those nostalgia filters on flashbacks in the movies. And who knows, maybe in twenty years, you'll be nostalgic for the way they look now. You could make it feel like that…" Haley said this carefully, but without any doubt in her voice.

Joe put his arm around her. "I don't know if I can make myself feel that way, but it's a nice way to look at it."

It was a short drive deeper into the foothills. Joe pulled off into a parking lot next to some picnic benches. He turned off the engine, and the headlights went out. It took a minute for

JD's eyes to adjust, but when he did, he could tell that the only reason he could see anything was from the light of the stars and the tiny sliver of a moon, now high in the sky. Joe sat at the picnic table, but faced outward, resting on his arms behind him with his head leaned back facing the stars. Everyone else followed his lead.

It was magnificent. Joe pointed up towards a long cluster of stars like a river across the blackness. "That's the Milky Way," he explained. "Our galaxy. Filled with trillions and trillions of stars, some even bigger and brighter than our own sun. This is a great night for this too because the moon is almost empty."

Dawn laughed. "Empty?"

"You know, not full?"

"I know what you mean, it's just funny!"

Joe smiled, and JD could see the deep creases in his cheeks even more than before.

"I don't know if you guys are enjoying the sounds of nature or whatever, but I would love a song right now," Haley said.

Dawn laughed. "Honestly, me too. I don't really know what the vibe is," Dawn said, scrolling through the music on her phone. "Sara, don't you have a stargazing playlist or something?"

"Something like that," Sara replied, pulling out her phone. "I'll play it and let me know if it's the vibe."

"I'm sure it is," Dawn said.

JD watched Sara's screen as she pulled up her rooftop playlist. JD could already see that she'd changed the title to, "Neon Lights and Natural Satellites." JD smiled as a bouncy, guitar intro started playing from the speaker of her phone. She placed it on the table, and everyone resumed looking up at the wild, starry expanse.

After a long minute, Joe said to Haley, "Remember when you said I don't gawk at the stars every night?"

"Mmhmm."

"Well, you're right, but I think I should."

"I think everyone should," Haley said resolutely.

No one said anything for a while. They let the music play up and out into the speckled sky, and watched as the stars twinkled modestly, yet all together in an impressive display all their own.

"So? What do you guys think? Who's buying pizza?" Joe said, suddenly.

"Wait, just like that?" Haley asked. "No final rebuttals? No closing remarks?"

"Nope." Joe and Haley looked to Dawn first.

"Hey, I'm still wondering how I got caught up in all this. And why do I have to go first?"

"You're right. I don't want answers to be swayed by another." Joe stated. "Heads down."

Dawn rolled her eyes, but everyone obeyed.

"Raise your hand I win the debate," Joe asks.

"Wait," Dawn interrupted, muffled by her arm in her face. "Can you say it based on the argument? Like the actual wording of what you guys are saying?"

"Good idea." Joe cleared his throat dramatically. "Raise your hand if you think the natural, celestial bodies of the universe, including every star in the night sky, the planets, and the moon are more—"

"Wait, you get the moon?" Haley interjected.

"Well, yeah. There's no way you're getting it in this argument." Joe looked to the group. JD and the others looked up. Dawn was nodding.

Haley scrunched her face together for a moment before conceding. "Alright, I think that makes sense."

"Alright," Joe gestured for everyone to close their eyes, and they did. "Raise your hand if you think the stars, planets, and the moon are more awe-inspiring than the man-made fireworks, neon signs, and city lights."

JD flinched to raise his hand, but hesitated. He knew all night that he'd vote on Joe's side, but something held him back. In his head, he knew that he should vote for the stars, but JD couldn't help but think about the echoing crackle of the firework display, or the soft lavender buzz of the neon OPEN sign. Something held him back from raising his hand.

Joe's voice broke in, "And raise your hand if you're voting for the man-made things."

JD slowly raised his hand. He opened his eyes to everyone looking at him. Haley was agape yet still grinning.

"Not gonna lie," Dawn said. "Didn't see that coming."

"Me neither," Haley said, "But I'll take JD's vote as a win for me."

"You're still buying the pizza though because Dawn and Sara have an ounce of sense." Joe joked.

JD shrugged, "It was a pretty convincing night."

Haley beamed again. "I will gladly buy that pizza."

"I'm so hungry," Dawn added.

Joe frowned looking at his phone, "Okay, bad news is that Cosmo's is definitely closed by now, but some other place might be open?"

"I refuse to eat any other kind of pizza," Haley announced.

"I didn't realize it was so late," Joe said, still looking at his phone.

JD spoke up, "Well if we're not attached to pizza, I know of a place with the best grilled cheese that never closes."

Joe looked up and grinned.

"We Don't Need Our Heads"
by A Great Big Pile of Leaves

The coffee shop was much quieter and less crowded than it was before. Joe led Dawn and Sara to a large corner booth, and JD followed Haley to the counter. The espresso machine bubbled and hissed, and soft, pleasant instrumental music played from the overhead speakers. Haley spent a minute grabbing jars of loose-leaf tea, smelling them, and replacing them on the shelf next to the register. "I think I'm going to get a tea for the table," she said to JD, still browsing. "Something without caffeine. Find one that smells nice."

JD grabbed a jar labeled 'Russian Blue' and smelled it. To his surprise, it smelled like blueberries and mint. He opened another one called 'Abyssinian' that smelled like black tea and cardamom. The barista had overheard Haley and said, "All the teas with orange stickers are herbal teas. They won't have caffeine."

Haley grabbed one with an orange sticker called, "British Shorthair." After smelling it, she smiled and passed it to JD. "What about this?" It smelled delicious, like orange and clove.

"That smells great," JD responded, "but where's the name come from?"

"They're all cat breeds. You either have to ask or smell it to know what you're getting."

The barista turned to them again. "Yeah, part of me wishes that we could just write the flavor on the jars too, but I think most of the regulars would riot."

"I'd riot," Haley said. "I find it so charming."

"Tell that to the morning rush," the barista said.

"Oh, that's fair."

"It is charming though. Even though I'm not a fan of cats." The barista tended to the espresso machine as it steamed. He was tall, even taller than Joe, and had a very well-kept, dark brown beard. It contrasted his messy, box-bleached head of hair in a lot of ways. He poured cream into the cup of espresso, and promptly took a sip. Foam was on his mustache when he asked, "You guys ready?"

"I think so," Haley said, noncommittally. We're going to get five grilled cheeses, and a pot of tea, but I haven't decided on the type."

The barista nodded. "I'll get those grilled cheeses going. My favorite herbals are the 'Cornish Rex' and the 'Maine Coon.'"

Haley smelled them both but decided on the 'British Shorthair.' She pulled out cash from her wallet and smirked. "Thanks, Levi," she said, under her breath. JD followed her to the table where Joe, Dawn, and Sara sat.

"Smelling all the tea again?" Joe asked.

"Yeah, and I picked the perfect one, so you're welcome."

"Thanks for paying for all of this, Haley," Sara said. "Sorry we voted against you."

Haley laughed. "I'll harbor resentment for the rest of my life. I'd like to thank my only friend, JD, for voting for me, and my worthy opponent for a riveting debate. And for driving all night."

Joe bowed slightly. "I'm just so excited. We went to Horsetooth. We're staying up all night. This is my favorite thing to do."

The barista arrived with a full platter of gooey grilled cheeses and a pot of tea. He set it down and said, "Thought I'd bring it out. You guys are the only ones here." When he looked up, his eyes met with Dawn's.

"Dawn?" he asked, hesitantly but visibly excited.

Dawn lit up.

"No way!"

Dawn stood up and met the barista with a hug. She leaned back and inspected him. "Look at your hair, you Kurt Cobain wannabe! I didn't know you worked here. How the hell have you been?"

"Yeah, I started last month. How are you?"

As the two of them continued talking, JD asked Sara how Dawn knew him, and she shrugged. Joe interjected, "We all went to high school together. Her and Alec were in a band together."

"Dawn was in a band?" JD asked.

Joe nodded, "They were good too."

"I didn't even know that," Sara added.

"She's mentioned it to me," Haley said, "but she never really talks about it."

"She played the trumpet and sang. It was awesome."

Dawn and Alec turned to the table, "Alec, you know Joe." They waved to each other and smiled. "This is Haley and Sara, my roommates, and our friend, JD." The introduction had warmed JD more than he'd expected. It was hard to imagine the fact that he'd met everyone that night.

"You should come jam with us sometime," Alec said to Dawn. "We haven't really found a band or anything, but Mel is still banging on the drums like their life depends on it."

At this, Dawn got quiet. "Maybe."

"Nevertheless, we should get coffee sometime. I feel like it's been years."

"I think it has."

"Well, lots to catch up on," Alec smiled as he said it. "I should get back to it, but it was great to meet you all. Good to see you, Joe." He and Dawn hugged before he left.

Dawn sat back down. She seemed somewhat sullen, but JD was burning with curiosity. "I didn't know you were in a band," he said, prompting her.

Dawn smiled weakly, "Oh yeah. It was fun."

"Did you guys write your own songs?"

Dawn scoffed. "Oh of course. We weren't some cover band; we were the real deal. Although we did do a pretty excellent 'Sweet Disposition' cover. It went pretty hard."

"What was your favorite thing you wrote?" JD asked.

Dawn looked at him and smirked. "I don't know. Nothing really comes to mind."

"My favorite was the one about the shipwreck. The one where you sang the whole time," Joe said.

Dawn threw her head back and groaned. "That one was so bad! I hate that you remember this." Dawn looked at JD, "Joe was our biggest fan."

Joe nodded. "I also liked the one about Laura?"

"That one was okay." Dawn smiled as she remembered. "We went through quite a long stint there sophomore year when everything was garbage."

JD looked at Joe, waiting for him to deny it, but he was looking at Dawn. She continued, "We really hit our stride junior year. We did the talent show that year. We were good."

"What changed?" JD asked. "Like, between sophomore and junior year?"

Dawn thought for a moment. No one said anything. "I think it's because we stopped taking everything so seriously. We were all really into music. We were big band geeks and thought we knew everything there was to know about music theory and all that." She paused and took a long sip of her tea. "Actually, I remember the day it changed for us. Or, at least for me. We were in Mel's basement, trying to write songs, but everything sucked. Nothing sounded good. It wasn't fun. Our band director had told us to write about what we love, but it wasn't working. It wasn't until Lee, who was as stoned as could be, mind you, picked up a can of orange soda that he was nursing and declared that he loved it. Like really in love with it. I remember laughing, but Lee didn't. He stared at it, with his bloodshot eyes and decided to write a song about it."

"Is this the same Lee from earlier? The story about the sign?" JD asked.

Dawn nodded. "We then all helped write this song together. It was, of course, called 'Orange Soda' and it was awesome. It was fun, and interesting, and didn't even end up being about soda—not really. I think that's what changed."

"Wait what? What changed?"

Dawn turned to JD, "We stopped worrying about writing what we thought would be good. When we wrote what we thought was the most musically correct, or lyrically profound, it sucked. We stopped writing songs about what we 'loved' and just wrote songs about what was right in front of us. They always ended up being about what we loved or cared about in the end, but somehow just better."

JD didn't know what to say; no one spoke. Dawn continued but looked only at her untouched grilled cheese. "Lee was always going on about the Muses. They are the Greek deities respons-ible for art and inspiration. Whenever we were stumped or in a rut, he would blame it on them. He said once that the Muses hide themselves in everyday objects and interactions, and the artist was someone that found them, or discovered them. I think he found one in that soda can that night and shared it with the rest of us."

Dawn looked up and saw that no one else had touched their food. "Oh my god, guys, eat!"

"I'd never heard that story before," Joe said.

"Well thanks for listening. I didn't realize I was rambling, and you guys weren't eating."

"I could listen to you ramble all night," Haley said, taking a bite.

"No, I hit my ramble quota for the night," Dawn said.

"But—"

"Ehp!" Dawn held her hand up to Haley.

"Fine."

As they continued eating, the song playing from the overhead speaker changed abruptly to a kind of easy-going rock song. Dawn looked up as it played to see Alec peeking out from the counter smiling.

"Is this what I think it is?" Dawn shouted at him.

"Hell yeah, baby! Best band alive!" Alec air-guitared and continued cleaning the espresso machine.

"We saw this band live together in high school," Dawn explained to the group. "I kind of forgot about them. We were so into them." Dawn looked at Alec as he worked. "Hey!" Alec turned around. "When are you and Mel jamming next?"

Alec beamed. "Literally, whenever you want."

"Cool. Sunday?"

He gave her two thumbs up.

"I'm rusty but I'm there. Also, JD is a songwriter," she gestured to JD. "He plays the French horn and the keys. I'll bring him too."

JD was visibly confused but was only met with a dramatic "rock on" hand sign from Alec. Dawn mocked him and continued eating.

JD looked at Dawn, "I don't know if the French horn is the right sound for a rock band, and I'm not a very good piano player."

"What about everything that I've said tonight makes you think I care that you're not the best classically trained piano player around?" Dawn raised an eyebrow.

JD nodded.

"Alec is a guitar god, and Mel was put on this earth to play the drums. They're both excellent musicians, but don't really fancy themselves songwriters. We'll need your expertise."

"I've never really written anything for a rock band," JD started, but Dawn shot him a look, "but I'm excited to!" he finished. Dawn nodded with approval, and they continued eating. The crew chatted about Cody and the party, and JD observed as he ate the grilled cheese. He tried to keep up with the lightning-quick banter around him, but his head was reeling with thoughts about writing music with Dawn's band. Whether he acknowledged it or not, JD had been slowly resigning himself to what his life would be like outside the music building; writing and playing music felt so out of reach. Without the composition classes, the concerts, even just the practice rooms, JD couldn't picture himself successfully writing anything. The idea of writing music with Dawn made JD swell with a kind of nerve-wracking excitement. He was giddy, sitting there, not at all listening to the conversation around him.

Outro:
"Arjun's Prelude"
by JD Miller

The drive back was quiet, and all the roads in town were empty. Joe broke the silence. "I'm already heading down Laurel; I think I'll take you guys home first, and then JD. Do you mind if I borrow your car until tomorrow? I don't really want to bike,"

Haley responded, "Oh yeah, that's fine. That's probably best too, I think Sara is already asleep."

In the backseat, Sara groaned softly, but didn't open her eyes.

When they pulled up to the house, JD could see the neon OPEN sign was still on, and it casted its purple hue onto the front lawn.

"We're getting brunch tomorrow," Dawn said to JD. "Make sure Joe gets your number." She yawned. "Although it will probably be midafternoon before we're all up."

Joe waited for everyone to get inside. He watched them turn off the sign, and he let out a dramatic sigh. JD moved to the front and Joe drove away.

"Thanks for inviting me tonight," JD said.

"I'm glad you came!"

"Sara and I were talking earlier. We're glad Haley forced us out."

Joe chuckled, "She's right about a lot of things. Even if I do fight her on most of them."

"What do you mean?"

Joe didn't say anything for a moment. "Well, I think I'm still right about the whole stars debate—I still haven't forgiven you for switching sides, by the way—but she might have a point. She says I'm too nostalgic, and I think she's right." Joe didn't look away from the road. "I don't think it's a bad thing to be nostalgic for something, but I admire Haley for how she looks at the world. I love that she makes the small things feel important."

JD didn't say anything. The rumble of the car, and the lack of music between them filled the space.

Joe continued, "She told me earlier that I romanticize last year too much. She's right that I don't do the things now that I loved about my freshman year. Dawn and I grew up here, and coming to college was the first time the city felt new—everything felt new. After what happened with my team in high school, I was so hungry to start over and to be somewhere else, and even though I'd lived here my whole life, college gave me that. It was exciting, and I felt adventurous. We'd stay up all night and drive around. We'd go for walks at midnight around campus. I met so many new people. A lot of me now wants that back, but I think Haley's right that my life isn't really that different. I can still do things that feel adventurous…" Joe trailed off. He looked at JD and smiled, "Tonight felt adventurous. It felt important."

JD nodded. He wanted to say that he agreed with Joe; the night had felt like an adventure. He also wanted to tell Joe that it was the first time college had felt that way, but he didn't want to admit it. "That sounds like a great first year of college," JD said.

"It was, but I can't help second guess that it's all in my head. Did your first year feel like that? You just finished yours," Joe asked.

JD almost laughed. He decided to be honest. "Not really. It was terrible."

"Really?"

JD nodded. "I spent every hour of it in a practice room. And not blissfully or charmingly so. I was bitter every time I picked up my instrument."

"You were bound to chuck that thing at someone eventually!" Joe jabbed.

JD groaned with embarrassment. Joe made a turn into a nearby neighborhood. He seemed to be driving in laps around the neighborhood roads near campus, and JD was grateful.

"I meant to ask earlier," Joe said, "but did you hear more from Arjun?"

JD shook his head. "I opened the envelope."

"Haley told me."

"I texted him an apology, but it was really late. He probably won't see it until the morning." JD thought again about the concert and pictured Arjun playing the solo without him there. It stung to think about. It felt like a horrible and ugly thing to leave someone with. "I just feel like a really shitty person. He called me selfish on the phone before we saw him. He's right."

Joe didn't say anything for a moment. "I—" he cut himself off, finding the words. JD let him. "I don't want to say too much," Joe said with his eyes still on the road, "I want Dawn to tell you, but I think you should know about tonight. Earlier, when Dawn played her trumpet in her room, it was the first time she'd played in a really long time." Joe paused, mulling the words over. "Her friend, Lee, was in a terrible car accident our senior year. It was bad, and he didn't make it. Dawn was really fucked up about it. I like to say that I'm her best friend, but really, he was. After it happened, Dawn stopped talking to her bandmates, and she hadn't picked up her trumpet since. Until tonight."

JD was silent. He thought about the stories Dawn had told him and about the song she'd played on her trumpet. He replayed in his head the way Dawn had picked up her trumpet and played the Stravinsky finale. He knew now that she was thinking about Lee. The song had been, in some way, a dedication to him. Dawn played for the crew to listen, but she played the song for Lee. JD thought about it more and decided that Dawn must have found a Muse. Whether it was in her trumpet, or even in the neon sign, JD didn't know. What he did know was that Dawn found it, and that it had been left for her by Lee to find when she was ready.

"I just thought you should know. Tonight felt like a big deal, and you were a big part of it."

JD nodded.

"And I hope you come to brunch tomorrow. Even if it is at 3pm." Joe passed JD his phone, and JD put his number into it. "I'll text you tomorrow when we wake up!" He waited for JD to get inside before driving off.

JD was exhausted but knew that he had one thing to do before the night ended. He bounded up the stairs to his dorm. From the pockets of his jeans, he taped together the song he'd written years ago. Then, under his wrinkled tuxedo, JD found his French horn still in its black case. With the taped-up song and his instrument in his hands, he left.

It wasn't yet sunrise; the stars were still in the sky, but they had begun to fade. JD practically jogged across campus with his eyes on the notes taped together. He sang the melody to himself and reminded his hands of the melodies and scales. He only stopped to catch his breath when he arrived at The Stump. He took a long deep breath before opening his case and retrieving his instrument. The golden brass seemed to glow in the white, fluorescent streetlights illuminating the plaza. He took one last look at the notes on the page, folded it, and put it in his pocket.

He stood on top of The Stump and looked around. He was alone, but he decided that he wouldn't care if he wasn't. He took another deep breath and felt the cold, early morning air in his lungs. He began to play. He played through 'Arjun's Prelude' as it was written—as a love song. He played it sweetly as he did for Arjun the first time. As the melody went on, JD thought about the good, intimate pieces he'd hoped he left with Arjun, and the beautiful pieces from Arjun that JD still held onto. He thought about their first kiss, that moment in the car at sunset. It stung to think about earlier in the night because it felt like a warm and beautiful thing that would never happen again. JD knew that that was true, it was just a memory now, but as he played, the memory felt cherishable. It felt like the kind of memory that makes it all worth it; like it was something worth dedicating music to. JD hoped the sweetness he felt for the memory was something Arjun could still feel as well.

The song had come to an end, but JD held the last note. He thought again about Dawn and how she played the Stravinsky. Something came to him. He played the song again from the beginning, but differently. He played it stronger and let the melody build and grow into something entirely its own. He played it less like a ballad or prelude, and more like a finale. It surprised JD how different the song had become—suddenly, yet naturally.

As JD played this second piece, he thought about the night he'd just had: the Fourth of July after his freshman year of college. He knew in that moment that he had made a night full of cherishable memories. A handful of beautiful, glowing things that were, for a night, right in front of him, and nowhere else in the universe.

JD had found a Muse. From where, he didn't know, but he could feel it as he played. He thought for a moment to stop playing and write down this new and bold melody, but he didn't. This song was for tonight, and JD wanted to play it for the night. He let the sound echo off the buildings around him; he let it careen and be swallowed up by the dark, early morning air above.

When the song finished, JD opened his eyes. The sun hadn't risen, but the stars had given way to its pale light still deep under the horizon. He looked up and pictured the songs he'd just played disappearing into space. He listened closely to the silence. At first, he wished the song ended with an applause; good performances deserve applause, but JD listened, and for some reason, loved hearing the emptiness, or rather the vastness all around him. There was something perfect about the silent stillness that surrounded him—something perfect about being able to savor the precise and bittersweet moment when one thing ends, and another begins. After another deep inhale, JD returned his instrument to its case and walked home.

Acknowledgements

Truly a million and one thank yous...

★ To Diondra Dilworth for teaching me the art of the playlist so many years ago.

★ To Hannah Drennen for always sharing her muses with me.

★ To Samantha Tovey for being the finest editor anyone could ask for.

★ To Tianna Zachariah for sharing her rooftop with me.

★ To my wonderful friends for reading the early copies and supporting me every step of the way.
A special thank you to Kaitlyn Phillips and Avery Jones; your annotated copies of the final draft are my most prized possessions.

★ To my family who I am so lucky to have.

★ To the artists and bands that inspired this playlist.

★ And to all the boys I've loved before, truly.

www.ingramcontent.com/pod-product-compliance
Lightning Source LLC
Chambersburg PA
CBHW070658010826
48975CB00014B/2531